KRSHN

Perplexed People Pleaser

Vedik Bobba

INDIA • SINGAPORE • MALAYSIA

ISBN 979-8-89026-967-6

Dedicated to the women of my life

My inspiring daughter

My intellectual wife

CONTENTS

FIRST TIME

"Cool down, cool down, cool down", whispered Krishna to himself while taking deep breaths. With shivering hands approaching the doorbell he took god's name and as he pressed the doorbell, within nanoseconds the door opened. Jayapradha had the same jitters and nervousness on the other side of the door while eagerly waiting for Krishna. While Krishna was trying to maintain his poise as he was entering the house, Jayapradha was trying to avoid direct eye contact. Her eyes were trying to scan him as much as possible while he was trying to scan her and the house thoroughly. She looked late-20s around 5'3" in height, wheatish, wore a kurti and pinned her hair. Her body language portrayed that she would be doing something apart from just sitting at home. She didn't tell him anything but, "sit down. Give me 5 minutes, I am winding up the kitchen". As he sat, he observed a small, kempt house with one bedroom. The hall had hundreds of books with shelves made to stick onto the ceiling as well. As he was scanning the house, he observed the television streaming one of his favorite songs; the hand-wound clock which his father used to wake up with every day; and the creaking cane sofa as he tried to reach one of the

Tamil books. As he was trying to guess what she would be doing, he heard from the kitchen, "I am a Tamil teacher and I teach at the school nearby".

After that he heard the final whistle of the cooker, some utensils getting washed, refrigerator door opening and closing, and some plastic covers being shuffled. As she brought a tray with two cups and said, "coffee", she was still trying to avoid the eye contact and so was Krishna. He was hesitant and denied, for which she didn't react and said, "give me a couple of minutes, I will change". As he was giving a quick read through the summary of the book the bedroom door opened. It was dark as all the curtains were closed; these were the thick ones with the lining that are typically found in the star hotels, so that made the room even darker. "Leave the TV on and come in", came the voice from the bedroom and as he entered, she was standing near the cupboard wearing a yellow spaghetti lace satin nighty, knee-length, with her breasts almost seen and unpinned hair. She was standing with both the legs and hands crossed and trying to look thru the corner of the eye. Both their hearts were pulsating fast, both were unable to look at each other straight and both were hesitantly coming close to each other. He removed his clothes, put on his condom, and came very close to her and smooched her. That was first time she looked straight into his eyes. There was shock and a flash of fear on her face. He got concerned and asked, "are you alright?" Her lips were trembling, and she started sweating. He got scared and held her tight over her shoulders and with a louder tone asked, "are you ok? shall I leave?". She said, "lets lie down".

Both were naked and he was lying on her trying to kiss her to create a mood. He had difficulty in trying to get his penis into her insides for over a minute and it was painful for both. She pushed him away and said, "lets have a drink to up our mood".

Jayapradha covered herself with a bedsheet, took out a key from the bedroom cupboard and told Krishna "get the vodka bottle from the secret drawer behind the books" pointing towards a book shelf. By the time he got the unopened bottle she was on bed with a mat and a tray on it with three bowls of snacks and two empty glasses and a juice bottle pouring out the juice in one glass. He had an awestruck expression on his face looking at her swiftness at work and told her, "you are supposed to pour the vodka first, measure and then pour the juice". She stared and said, "the juice is for you, and you are free to mix how much ever vodka you want to. I will have on the rocks with ice. Go and get some ice from the fridge". As he went to the small kitchen he was again awestruck as the kitchen looked unused. All pulses were in transparent bottles and in one shelf, there was a steel stand with different sized plates & bowls arranged as per their size. He didn't have any trouble in choosing the right sized bowl for the ice and the same organized arrangement was in the fridge as well. "Keep everything in its place and have a place for everything", thought Krishna.

When he entered with the bowl of ice and bottle of water, he was shocked to see that she had already completed around 90ml with juice and asked, "are you alright madam?". "Make an on the rocks for me again, make yours and start massaging my back", came an emotionless reply. As he took his first sip and was placing the glass on the mat, she gulped hers and placed on the mat at the same time. He didn't utter a word and started massaging her.

"I am the only child to my parents and completed my M.Ed. from Anna University. I am the first graduate in my family and my father is a bus conductor. He was looking out for a potential groom for me when I started working in this school. I was happy that my to-be-hubby was working in the same city in an IT company and his house was near to my school. Apart from this I was even happy that I wouldn't have any in-law issues. His mother passed away when he was young and his father saw our wedding from his death bed, passed away a week later; that was his last wish. And the best part was he was happy with me working. This is all we spoke when he came to see me. I didn't give it a second thought and gave a nod to my parents. We didn't go to any honeymoon after marriage as he had a busy work schedule then. He told me that he will take me to Andaman in a couple of months. But it's been eight months and he's always into work. Look, today on a Saturday afternoon he's in office. He leaves at 830 and is back at night 1030. After that he eats and sleeps. All that I know is he is working on some USA project, and he never tells me any details, no information on his friends at work or outside, he never calls me from work and only I end up calling him. I had my doubts on any extra marital affair, but I did my basic groundwork, following him to workplace and sometimes following back from workplace, but there is nothing I could find suspicious. But yes, he never lets me touch his phone. On Sundays he tells he is extremely tired and ends up sleeping for 8 hours during the daytime. And remaining time he genuinely works from home. I tried hugging him many times and we kissed each other many times but nothing happened beyond that. He would push me away. I gave him many indicators many times and as a matter of fact wore this nighty many times in front of him. But he is not at all interested in me. It's been 8 months now since we got married. Am I not looking good?". The last two sentences came with a louder questioning tone and that's when Krishna saw water droplets on the mat.

Both finished the vodka bottle by then and Jayapradha turned towards Krishna expecting an answer but how could he answer a rhetorical question like this from any woman. Krishna was thinking fast inside on whether to provide a philosophical answer like, "beauty lies in the eyes of the beholder" or "you are decent looking, and I don't see any issues in your looks". Just as he was about to open him mouth to reply, she kissed him. She kissed him forcefully and the intoxication due to vodka started kicking in for both, and this time it was an easy entry for him. Both moaned in ecstasy, surprisingly his voice louder than hers. Just after it got over, she told him shyly, "this is my first time, first time in my life, first time with a stranger". He replied with a smile, "this is my first time, first time in my life, you are my first client".

Krishna went to the loo and cleaned up first. He put his used condom in a small plastic cover and kept it in his bag, wore his clothes and shut the bedroom door behind so that Jayapradha could get ready. The coffee outside became cold and just as he started sipping the bedroom door opened. She was in the same yellow nighty with a towel over her shoulders. She pulled the cup from his mouth and said, "how can you have cold coffee? Let me heat it again for you". Krishna continued browsing the same book, Jayapradha changed into the same kurti and came back with two coffee cups. "Can I ask you a personal question?" asked Krishna hesitantly as he was sipping his coffee. "Do you think your husband is gay?".

Jayapradha was shocked to hear this. Krishna immediately turned the television off. She paused sipping her coffee and stared at Krishna. He became conscious and said, "sorry, I don't mean to get into your relationship with him", Jayapradha cut him short and started raising her voice, "what do you mean, how is it possible, what the hell are you telling?". Krishna started calmly, "please hear me out for a minute calmly. See from what I have observed, you are trying your best to entice him and make your moves towards him. I see you as an organized & planned person; the way you have kept the house and the kitchen, the way you arranged the mat and glasses, and finally the way you smartly put the coffee on the gas and then changed so that time doesn't gets wasted. You have a place to keep your cupboard key and you have smartly utilized the ceiling space in this small house to have your books shelves which I guess you have done after marriage. So basically, you are someone who knows what you want out of life and looks like you have planned for something in the near future as well, both from your personal and professional point of view. You are the first graduate, your father is also trying hard to make ends meet, you are also working; so, you are in a better position to understand your husband's work life, which is very good. Also looks like your husband is a teetotaler, that's why you have hidden the bottle. And he's genuinely busy at work, trying to make big in his career and at the same time not talking about his friends at work or college and very careful about his phone. Have you observed him talking with his friends over phone outside the house whereas he has no problem in taking office calls at home?"

Jayapradha's eyes went wide open and was unable to come to terms on the first question Krishna asked. She put the coffee cup on the table and sank into her hands. Krishna just got up briefly to touch her over her shoulder but sat down. She was processing whatever Krishna told and after a long pause still with her head in her hands said, "Ramarajan. Ravi mentions about his office friend Ramarajan a lot. He is so smart, he is so talented, I have been to his room many times, after work I go to his room and learn more about work from him, he has his own freelancing apart from work wherein he takes small projects from his friends in the USA. I also help him with that and get extra income. He is single and doesn't want to get married, but his parents are forcing him". She looked at him and said in a slow tone, "I am shocked, whatever you said may be true. I don't know what to do. My parents will not understand this. Whom do I go and tell, he has no parents to complaint to. What do I do?". Meanwhile Krishna completed his coffee and said calmly, "Look, there is nothing wrong in being a homosexual. Ravi is not doing this on purpose or voluntarily. Please understand that it is completely natural. Many animals exhibit homosexuality. It is just that these people are differently wired inside their head. That doesn't mean we should look down upon them or discard them from our society. Left-handedness is also something similar, these people are differently wired, their brain tells them that their left hand is dominant. It is important to recognize this as a few people don't know that they are gay and are confused. These people need help from straight people like us and not be shooed away".

Jayapradha was slowly trying to get her senses back together as Krishna took out two cigarettes from his bag and asked, "Do you smoke?" She got up and got the smallest plate Krishna ever saw and handed over to him and said "ashtray". She took one from his hand and lit it with his lighter, sat down and started scratching her head. She took deep puffs inside and let it thru her nose. Krishna was quietly observing her as he smoked and didn't utter a word. She pointed at his bag and asked, "do you have a drink in that bag?". Krishna took out a whiskey bottle and kept on the table. He got up and got the glasses and bottles from the bedroom and got ice from fridge, and as he started pouring the drink said, "please don't mix drinks madam as…", she cut him short and said, "give me three more cigarettes and make me a stronger drink". For the next thirty minutes both didn't utter a word. He had only one drink and was attempting to read the book and at the same time observing her. He tried hard to make a conversation, but she didn't look at him. She finished his bottle too and all the three cigarettes, kept pacing in the hall, went to the kitchen a couple of times to have water, pulled her hair occasionally and kept murmuring something to herself. At the end of thirty minutes she wailed, "my parents married me to a gay". "Why do you blame your parents when you are the one who gave them the nod?" pat came the reply calmly. She got wild and picked up the bottle to hit him but controlled herself and sank into the sofa. Krishna told himself to keep his mouth shut and decided to leave. He checked his bag and got up to leave. She told him politely, "sorry, please sit" as tears rolled down her eyes. "What do you want me to do? Divorce him, complaint to the cops, tell my parents, I am confused", asked Jayapradha calmly.

Krishna understood that she has calmed down and said, "Ok, relax. First, you need check if Ravi is really a homosexual. Also, you need to please read up on this. Given your interest in reading it should be a cakewalk for you. Please try to understand that he is a left-hander whereas majority of them like you and me are right-handers. This can be understood as simple as this. There is no need to go to cops or tell your parents now. Since you said he is not at all interested in talking to you, try to see if you can catch him red-handed". She thought for a moment and said, "can you please help me with this?". Krishna never expected this. He didn't answer. She came to him and held his hands and said, "you can do this as Ravi will never know that he is being tracked". Krishna took a long pause, put on his bag, and stood up and said, "ok I will help. Now I must leave, so please pay me". "Do I have to pay twice since it didn't work the first time," asked Jayapradha questioningly. Krishna smiled and said, "just pay me ₹3000" and opened the main door to leave. Jayapradha said, "hey wait, you didn't tell me anything about yourself". With one hand on the doorknob and other carrying the bag, Krishna smiled and said, "since we will anyway meet again, lets keep it for the next time". "Please shave, it pokes", smiled Jayapradha. Just as Krishna closed the main door he winced and thought, "shit, I forgot Karthik's first point".

Chapter 2

GENESIS

Krishna, aged 27, was born and raised in Chennai. Being an only child of working parents, he did not end up being excessively pampered or with a wide friend's circle. His father worked in the public works department and his mother was an administrative staff in a private hospital. Staying in the busiest part of the town, T.Nagar, he became accustomed to the hustle and bustle of a crowded city. For the same reason, though he enjoyed the company of his cousins whenever he went to his village in the summers, he couldn't stay for more than a couple of weeks. He always had a good rapport with the other gender. All his ten cousins were females, five each on his father's side and mother's side. He used to flaunt about this with his friends always. All of them were married except the youngest sister on his mother's side. In all their marriages a standard photo-op was he sitting in the middle with his two sisters near his knees, two sisters near his shoulders and the eldest one behind him, and all of them would ensure that they would wear the same color attire. Though the distances have increased between all of them over time, their summers meet at their village has moved to the New year with his father's side cousins as most of them are outside India; and Deepavali with his mother's side cousins as most of them are in Chennai itself. This was rigorously practiced every year so that they don't miss out on their camaraderie. Apart from that, he kept in touch with them over a call and exchanging anniversary wishes and birthday wishes over Whatsapp was a routine.

Krishna has always been grateful about his education as he studied from the best school in the city, and it featured on the national news as the India's best school a couple of times. He is still in touch with his school friends and occasionally gets to hang out with them in a club in Adyar where one of his friend's is a member. Today half of them are outside India as it is atypical with the students from this school. Krishna was also a movie buff and ensured he would catch up with at least three movies a month. His favorite star was Sushant Singh Rajput. He was enamored by Sushant's charisma on screen and off screen, considering how a small-town boy became big and looked up to him as his inspiration. Sushant's photo was his display picture on Whatsapp. He completed his bachelors in mechanical engineering, from Chennai. After completing his Masters in the USA, he was hell bent on getting a core engineering job unlike many others who switched to the IT side. When he informed his parents that he would return from the USA, he had many fights with his father. Krishna's father was completely furious with Krishna's decision of coming back as he was under the impression that many of his colleagues' kids were well settled with good jobs and earned well but how come Krishna couldn't make it in the USA. Initially when Krishna was back the fights were on a weekly basis. But seeing

Krishna at home and thinking that he was not serious about his life, the fights became a daily agenda. It was a difficult situation for all the three at home. It was getting too much for Krishna to handle and so he moved out of the house.

Krishna, on the other hand was trying to start something on his own after coming back. Given his experience abroad, he had many ideas on improving the existing processes and making things more efficient. He was self-made, he managed his daily expenses with his savings from USA as he was getting decently paid as a teaching assistant. He started a small ten-table restaurant in Adyar with another college friend of his, Vivek. Vivek's father met with an accident once and Krishna donated blood as both their groups matched. So, both Vivek and his father felt indebted and helped Krishna with this restaurant. Vivek's father had many businesses and so investing in this restaurant was a no-brainer. Krishna learnt everything on the job and struggled for the first one year. At the end of the first eight months losses piled up but since Vivek knew that it was first time for Krishna, he gave it more time. More so Vivek barely had time to support Krishna as he was busy with his father's businesses. Krishna was a data crazy person and believed that if the data is interpreted correctly then there is a scope for improvement. He even captured data such as which customer sat on which table and at what time did the water cans get delivered. Vivek didn't even have time for the financials and so told Krishna not to bother on such irrelevant data, but Krishna continued tracking for his own satisfaction. He didn't give up easily, learnt from his mistakes and set things right in the next few months. After that he only had to manage the restaurant for a few hours in the day as they started making profits. Krishna saved enough over the next three months and bought his favorite bike, Bullet.

It was a Sunday afternoon, and his restaurant was beaming with customers. Krishna was busy checking the stock in the kitchen as there was a concern from a customer about a non-availability of a chicken dish and at the same time there was leakage of a water pipe in the kitchen. Krishna was making frantic calls to the nearest available plumber as customers had a difficult time to wash their hands. He was busy in the kitchen trying to fix the pipe, but he knew nothing could happen as the piping had to be replaced but given his interest in engineering he was trying for a workaround. He heard a loud voice, "where's my chicken biriyani, I have been waiting for twenty minutes". He signaled to his staff to attend to that lady immediately, but his staff didn't move. As he was pondering about this familiar voice, he heard again, "where's your manager, I need to talk immediately. Is this how you make customers wait?", the voice became sterner. He starred at his oldest staff Charlie, while trying to come up with a solution for the water leakage. He was surprised to see Charlie smiling. He turned and scanned this girl from the bottom as he was bending away from the pipes; to see this thin tall girl with black slippers, black shorts, black T-shirt, and black color spectacles, squirmed to himself, "shit, Abhinaya". He immediately left everything and without washing his greasy hands walked towards her. He was angry at her, but she had an angry look on her face as well. All customers were waiting to see what would happen next. He knew that she was way too smart and couldn't shout back at her. He came to her and said, "Madam please wait for ten minutes, your order will be ready". She maintained her same tone and said, "but I have been waiting for twenty minutes. How will you compensate me?". He was feeling embarrassed as people were still starring at both. He quickly tried to manage the situation by offering water to the customers waiting at the table near him and as he moved away from the table, showed his frustration to Abhinaya, and whispered, "why are you creating a scene"? She replied with the same tone, "hello, I am asking you, how will you compensate me?" He understood that it is very difficult to win against her now in this situation as people didn't stop starring at them. "Madam, I am the manager here, I apologize for delay, but please note that your order will be ready in ten minutes", said Krishna calmly. She immediately replied, "ok fine, if it is not ready by ten minutes then I will come back again". As she turned to walk away, he walked past her towards the table beyond her and whispered to her in the ear, "please fuck off".

Krishna immediately attended to all customers personally explaining the situation. All of them went back to their discussions. As he attended the table where a few college boys sat, he could overhear them telling amongst themselves, "god save the guy she marries", and all of them started laughing. There was a small smile on Krishna's face. The first thing he did was to ensure Abhinaya's order was ready in the next ten minutes. The plumber had come in the meantime and was attending the issue. He ensured that the relevant masala and the chicken reached the restaurant in the next one hour so that the stock is replenished. As he was checking his accounts, Charlie kept the chicken biriyani box on his desk and smiled as he pointed towards the box, there was a 'Sorry' note pasted on the box. Charlie always kept post-it notes handy in the storeroom as this was not the first time Abhinaya created a melodrama. He also knew that she does it on purpose many times, but Krishna never gets irritated with her. He knew that Krishna had a special place for her. "I will take it and go, else she will screw all our happiness", told Krishna.

Abhinaya was in her car with the air conditioning in full speed and crooning to a song from the radio, shaking and moving her hands in the air. Krishna opened the door, gave her the biriyani and as he was about to vent his frustration, she placed her left hand on his mouth and put her right index finger on her lips. Then she started eating her biriyani, crooning to the song, and started nodding her head. He turned down the air conditioning and the radio volume and said calmly, "Abhi, how many times have I told you not to insult me in front of customers or staff? Doesn't it get into your head?" "Why is the leg piece not fresh today? I have been telling you to do a maintenance check for the last 2 months. Why do always make sure you wait till the stock is over? Why can't you maintain a minimum stock trigger in your system? And when will you genuinely give me a sorry card instead of Charlie? So, when all this nonsense is happening you expect me to come and cuddle you in your restaurant?" Abhinaya told all this casually as she was munching her food. Krishna kept staring at her and couldn't utter a word as she always knew how to corner him at the right moment. He didn't know what to tell and she continued, "when did we last go out for a long drive? When did you last get me my favorite box of chocolates? When did you genuinely take me out to a nice candlelight dinner?" and started giggling. Krishna kept his hand on his head and said, "Abhi, look I am sorry, I will be proactive from now on", she cut him short and said, "look I am almost done, lets go now for a movie, Interstellar, I heard it is good. Then we can go for a bowling game and have dinner and then go home".

Krishna pleaded to Abhinaya, "look it's a Sunday afternoon and the restaurant will be busy till the night, there is lot of pending work, and I cannot just leave", Abhinaya didn't allow him to complete, opened the door and shouted, "Charlie anna". Krishna put his hands on his head. "Hi Charlie anna, how are you? How are your kids doing? Look your boss is not taking me out on the weekend. Please teach him some manners on how to treat women", giggled Abhinaya. Krishna folded his hands and said, "Can you give me 5 minutes?". Krishna went to the restaurant while Abhinaya continued her chat with Charlie. Krishna gave some instructions to his staff, made some calls and asked Charlie to call if there is any urgency. "Charlie anna, you know that I am the one who is going to pick up the call when his phone rings right?" said Abhinaya as she faked a laughter. Krishna smiled at her and said, "there is some magic in you that I just can't get angry with you, lets go. Oh, by the way, before I forget, my chronic stomach pain which I mentioned is gone and am feeling much better, looks like the third doctor's medication has worked". "That's my baby", giggled Abhinaya and pulled his right cheek, and then drove the car towards the theatre. Both had a good time at their favorite theatre, Satyam Cinemas. They had a craze to take selfies with a particular pose for every movie they saw, wherein both mimicked their fingers to be horns on each other's heads and took this picture in front of the movie poster. After that they skipped the idea of bowling alley and went to the bar at a star hotel. Abhinaya ran thru the menu and ordered for two long island iced teas for herself. She looked at Krishna and asked, "what do you want?". As Krishna leaned towards her to pick up the menu, she told the waiter, "two pineapple juice, no sugar, no ice". He smiled and asked her, "then why did you ask me? But hold on, why two drinks?". "Because I know you will look thru the whole menu and order for the same juice, because you don't drink and drive and because I know you like pineapple and because I know you will not have a problem with me having two drinks"., told Abhinaya in a rhythmic tone. "But I could always try something else today right". "No, not today, because I need to tell you something important", said Abhinaya with her eyes rolling over. "So, let me guess, are you pregnant?", asked Krishna doubtingly.

"Nooo", she felt shy and pushed Krishna away, "something bigger than that. We have decided to get married, Abdul and I, and you know what, he said he will come over here now to meet you", giggled Abhinaya. Krishna faked a laughter and said, "thank god I don't need to handle you from now on. Good that I can hand over the burden of 55kg to someone else. Do you remember the college guys at the table today afternoon? I know you do, you have a super sharp memory. They were also telling the same thing - god save the guy she marries". She pulled his ears and by then the waiter had come with the drinks; and Abdul also arrived. All of them exchanged their greetings, Krishna sat a bit away from both and looked at Abdul and said, "I am really really happy for both of you, she told me just now. Its been what, three years now since you have been together, I am really really happy for you". Abdul smiled and replied, "she said that you will always be the first person to know every decision of hers and that's how it has been this time as well". Krishna replied, "so from now please handle this burden well. She's the last sister remaining to get married". Krishna was surprised that Abhinaya was quiet and looked into her eyes to see what she was thinking. She had tears in her eyes and was controlling them. At that moment Krishna had tears too. She immediately said, "lets dance", while taking a sip. "Sure, come on Krishna", said Abdul. Krishna denied as he was tired and saw them go to the dance floor and momentarily shut his eyes.

Abhinaya is Krishna's mother's sister's daughter, the last girl waiting to get married. They stayed in the next street in T.Nagar. So, both Abhinaya and Krishna grew up together. Both had common friends and they used to stay at each other houses for weeks together, so they had to stock their clothes in both the houses. Abhinaya was a child prodigy. She could solve a Rubik cube under ten seconds when she was eight years old. She was always the class topper throughout and had an extremely sharp memory. She won most of the elocution competitions during her school at all the inter-school events, was the school pupil leader, voracious reader of fiction and often helped Krishna during the exams. She was a reserved person and since she was always into studies, she didn't bother much about her health or her looks. She weighed 85kg and never wore anything but salwar all her through her life. She did her Computer Science engineering from IIT Madras, and tragedy struck her during her final year on her birthday. Her father was working in merchant navy and was barely at home. Her mother taught math tuition at home. After one of her father's trips was over, he took Abhinaya out lunch. She questioned him about why her mother was not coming for which he said he had to talk something personal with her. After the lunch got over, as they entered the car, he confided to her that he liked someone from his team and wanted to divorce her mother. Abhinaya cried badly and didn't know whether to be angry with her father or be sad for him. She never heard of divorce in her family. She kept crying till they reached the house and her father told her to convey this to her mother.

As she entered the house and lied down in her room, she texted Krishna and told him to meet her immediately. Her mother came inside and asked Abhinaya to take her out to shopping. She did not know how to reveal this message to her mother. Both went on the bike on errands and completed a lot of work. Abhinaya's mother wanted to have her favorite snacks, so they stopped and ordered for a takeaway. As they were waiting on their bike for the parcel, two guys with helmets came and stopped close to them and the guy in the front asked for directions. As Abhinaya was trying to explain, the guy in the back took out a bottle and splashed it on her face. As she was trying to indicate directions her right hand came in between and bore the brunt of the acid. Some of it burnt her right cheek, right ear, and hair. Most of the acid fell on her mother. The sudden pain made her loose balance of the bike, and both the mother and daughter fell. The bike fell on her left leg and got fractured. Her mother fell hard in such a manner that her left temple landed on a sharp stone. The guys on the bike fled immediately. As they had planned this earlier, they chose to ride in the opposite direction so that they would not be chased. But fate turned out to be against them; they lost control, fell on the ground and got ran over by a water tanker; both died on the spot. Police later informed that the acid incident was a case of mistaken identity, the guys planned to throw acid on another girl.

Abhinaya and her mother were rushed to the hospital. Her father took note of the situation and met Abhinaya first and started crying. He told Abhinaya that her mother had an internal head injury and there was no chance of a surgery to save her and started crying. He asked her if she had a chance to talk to her mother. Abhinaya cried badly and told him to take her to her mother. Her mother was asleep, Abhinaya held her hands and told her father without looking at him, "let her not know anything, let her assume that you loved her, let her die peacefully dad, and you please remain guilty for the rest of your life". Abhinaya got discharged a week later. She barely spoke to him that week. She realized that all her life she lived in a cocoon and the reality that she lost her parents in a day had brought a paradigm shift in her personality. She took special permission from the college, and they had no qualms in giving her an off for the final semester as she was a college topper as well. She employed a full-time maid at home, hit the gym every day and lost 30kg. She changed her wardrobe completely to western. When she went for her campus placement many had a tough time in recognizing her. The girl who had never been to a parlor and the girl who never wore a jeans in her life and the girl who never waxed her hands or legs had a complete makeover. All heads turned towards her and the boys who never saw her ever, could not take their eyes off her. She landed with a plush job from one of the Big 4 consulting firms. She traveled throughout the week and was at home only during certain weekends.

Krishna's fights with his father were only getting worse as he was not employed, and his father was completely upset over this. The big fight happened on a Saturday night. His father compared him with all his friends' children, then the comparison grew to his office colleague's children and then to his relatives' kids abroad. Abhinaya just entered the Krishna's house at that time. She wore a camisole with a shrug and shorts. She just started trying to explain to Krishna's father and he started shouting at her. He told her that her life was perfect as even if she would have got married by now it wouldn't matter much as her father earned enough because of his work. She was also a college topper and had a plush job. She tried keeping her cool and explaining to him that Krishna will make it big and only needs time. He yelled her, "who are you to tell that. What kind of clothes do you wear? People who wear such clothes only talk like this otherwise if you were like before you would have also drilled some sense into this jobless guy". She shouted back at him, "what has my dress got to do with this conversation? And in which world is it written that people who were one kind of a dress talk in a particular manner. Uncle, I think you are completely stressed, and you need to relax". He shouted back to her, "get out of my house and you have no right to interfere in my family matter". That's when Krishna got wild and said, "Enough. Enough is enough. Dad you better apologize to her. She's trying to help you and me have a good conversation and you are only worsening it. I am done staying here. I am moving out". His father lost his cool and screamed, "Get lost. Go and beg and stay on the roads. Only then you will realize my value". Abhinaya calmed down and said, "Krishna, you will stay with me from now".

After both these incidents both supported each other very well. Krishna visited Abhinaya every day at her house after her accident. He drove her to gym daily, took her out to her favorite movies and made her favorite dishes with the help of the maid. That's when he started getting interested in the idea of a restaurant. He met his friend Vivek and came up with the idea of a restaurant. As things were getting finalized, he wanted to inform his parents but that's when all hell broke loose on that dreadful Saturday night. He decided that he would take up a room in Adyar closer to the restaurant. But Abhinaya's offer was better as she was just starting her work and since it involved extensive travel, she would not be available during weekdays, and she also wouldn't be in Chennai on all weekends. As time progressed Abhinaya was visiting Chennai only once a month. That was her rest time at home and Krishna ensured that she was given home cooked food only unless asked for. He also ensured that he had adequate stock of vodka as it was their favorite drink. After a couple of years Abhinaya confessed to Krishna about Abdul and Krishna was overjoyed hearing it.

"Hey Krishna wake up", said Abhinaya. Krishna for a moment didn't realize where he was. "How come you can sleep while sitting, please teach me", giggled Abhinaya. As he got up Abhinaya fell on him and showed three fingers and winked. He told Abdul that he would drive her home. As she sat in the car, the radio was playing her favorite song, she turned it off and closed her eyes, pinched her skin between her eyes, and told Krishna in a serious tone, "Krishna, now itself you are lonely, and you will feel more so after I get married. We have not decided whether we will stay in this house at T.Nagar or move to his apartment on OMR. Whether I am here in this house or not it doesn't matter, stay with me till you find someone for yourself. And listen to me," he looked at her for a moment while driving but her eyes were still closed as she continued pinching the skin between her eyes, "please find someone for yourself. It is better in many many ways. I know what loneliness means, don't ever feel that way", and she had tears.

Krishna knew that Abhinaya was missing her mother. She barely spoke to her father after he settled with his new partner. Both reached home and he carried her all the way from the car till the house, like carrying a rice sack. He dropped on her bed, and she slept like a baby. He went to the hall and got some vodka, played the television, and started browsing the newspaper. He came across an article that caught his attention wherein it was mentioned about a guy who lost his job and became a gigolo, and later got caught by his wife. Some random thoughts came into his head, "what this guy would have been doing every day, what kind of women would he have slept with, what kind of emotions would he have gone thru?" He read more about this escort service on the net and became more curious. He came across a few websites that had mobile numbers of these guys. He noted down a few numbers and slept. The next day he went to the restaurant and called the first number which was turned off, the second one was out of coverage area and the third one got picked up immediately within the first ring. Krishna said, "hello, is this Karthik? This is Krishna, I came across your number on a website". The husky voice from the other said, "yes, this is Karthik, but I don't do gay sex". Krishna apologetically said, "Sorry Karthik, I am not interested in gay sex, but I would like to meet you once. I am a journalist and since I am writing an article, I would like to talk you for thirty minutes". There was a long pause, then Krishna said, "sorry Karthik, I can't hear you, maybe I will repeat myself. I am not…", Karthik cut him short and said, "meet me at the bar in Mylapore at 730 today, I will send the address" and the call ended. Krishna had all kind of thoughts going inside his head; whether Karthik would turn up, whether he was taking the right decision, whether he was interested in becoming a gigolo for some time in his life, why did he even make that call, everything in his life was going smooth except for a life partner, would he find someone special thru this.

Krishna was always punctual wherever he went. He felt that it was important to respect other's time, no matter who the other person is as the other person is taking out personal time for him. Krishna ordered for a pineapple juice as he had to drive back. As he was watching others on the tables around him, he got a pat on the back and there was this thin tall wheatish guy behind him who said, "Krishna?". Krishna replied slowly, "Hi Karthik, please sit. What would like to have?". Karthik asked the waiter for a beer without looking at the menu and Krishna said, "Look Karthik I will be honest with you. I am not a journalist, and I am not writing an article. I want to become a gigolo and need your advice on this". Krishna didn't know how he had the courage to tell this, but the words just spurted out of his mouth. Karthik showed his frustration and replied immediately, "is this a joke? What the hell are you talking about?". Krishna replied calmly, "I am sorry, but I wanted to be upfront with you, if you don't want to continue this conversation you can leave. I will pay for the beer". By that time the waiter came with the glass and asked Karthik to check for the chillness. Karthik indicated to the waiter to pour the beer. After the waiter left, Karthik took a couple of sips, took out a pack of cigarettes and gestured to Krishna if would like to smoke.

Both went outside and took a few puffs and that's when Karthik started to talk, "look, I gave it a deep thought. You can take all my calls that I am getting. I will forward the numbers to you. I broke my own rule, never get emotional. I got in love with a lady who genuinely likes me. We have decided to move to Dubai with her son. Her husband left her for another woman". Krishna was listening to every word carefully. Both went inside and Karthik continued, "you have the same body structure as mine so that's a good advantage. Hit the gym and start working out, it will help, especially focus on your lower body and thighs. There are three main rules; first, always take the money before starting. Second, be prepared how to react if the frustrated husband suddenly knocks the door when you are in action as he forgot his spectacles, or an irritating neighbor comes and asks for a leaf of spinach. And the third main thing which I broke, never get emotional or personal. Everyone has hundreds of problems and women have this talent of crying at the drop of a hat and venting out their frustrations on why their husbands are cheating them or why their husbands are mad behind money and work outside the country or why their husbands keep beating them for no reason. You have gone for a purpose, finish the purpose and come back".

Krishna was in full attention. Both repeated their drinks and went for another smoke. Karthik continued, "try to see the situation and act accordingly. Some women would want some foreplay, some would want you to have a hard-on immediately whereas some would want you to take it slowly. Expectations vary from person to person. Coming to protection, wear two condoms as you never know when you can impregnate someone as chances of a condom getting torn is possible. Also try to see if you can verify the number, verify the source, try to recce if you feel it is sounding suspicious; see all this is subjective and depends on how lucky you are", smiled Karthik. "Now moving on to the don'ts. Don't overeat and go, there are high chances that you will have to shit after you are done. Don't take too many liquids as you may want to piss when you have a hard-on but at the same time the lady would be in an all-time high and you cannot leave a customer unsatisfied. So, at that moment you will not be able to ejaculate, and the semen will remain in your penis and could cause pain. Don't leave any evidence".

Krishna stared at Karthik, as he continued, "no socks, no shoes, no shirts, no belt, no watch, no ring, no bracelet, no chain, no jeans. Wear something that is easy and fast to remove and wear. Again, no evidence." Krishna was wondering why he was telling all this as Karthik continued, "see in case you have run away from a situation you have to be prepared. And all these accessories are unnecessary evidence against you if you forget them in the house". Krishna became a little cautious and asked slowly, "what are the chances that we get caught by police?" Karthik laughed loudly and said, "of course the chances are high. Prostitution is illegal". Krishna looked around to check if anyone heard them. Karthik continued, "till now I have not been caught and I am lucky. Your bad luck can get you caught in the first time itself. See I am having a good conversation talking to you. I have decided to leave and am going to give all my leads to you. You are fortunate as you will not have any advertising expenses. So, you decide and tell me". Krishna had a confused look on his face and didn't know what to answer; his thoughts came back again; was he doing the right thing, why did he even make this call at the first place, why did he even come here, was he sure he wanted to become a gigolo, what will happen if he gets caught, how will he face his relatives, parents, and Abhinaya. Karthik continued, "Obviously I don't expect an answer today. You can take a few days. But one thing, don't regret your decision later in life. Be honest with your decision". Krishna paid the bill, and both left.

Krishna got busy the next couple of days with the restaurant and suddenly there was a call during lunch time from Karthik. Krishna hesitantly picked up the phone and Karthik said, "what happened no reply?". Krishna was thinking hard what to reply, he wanted more time as he didn't give this much of a thought after the meet in the bar. Krishna just opened his mouth to reply and heard, "there's this woman who called me for tomorrow afternoon". It was a Saturday afternoon and Krishna's restaurant would be busy. His staff would need him for support and as he was thinking fast on what to reply and Karthik said, "Hey Krishna, can you hear me?" Immediately Krishna replied, "ok send me the details" and kept the phone down. Krishna mind was running with different thoughts; did I make a mistake, what have I decided to do, am I going to be caught by the police, what are the chances that I would contract AIDS. "How much", asked one customer by coming over to his desk. Krishna was still lost in thought. "How much", this time the customer asked loudly. He replied blankly, "3000". The customer was shocked and raised his voice, "I had only biriyani, what are you saying?" "Sorry sir, its 180", said Krishna as he came back to his senses, checked the bill again if he was telling the correct amount and thought to himself that that's what he would get tomorrow for his service.

Chapter 3

ENDEAVORS

After Jayapradha, Krishna became more aware on what is required for himself and what is needed to get updated for this kind of a service. He called Karthik, thanked him and told him to continue to send his leads. He got a bag with a lock and a secret compartment, ensured he bought condoms of different flavors from different pharmacies and always stacked his bag with alcohol and cigarettes. He started hitting the gym with specific focus on lower body and thighs. As per Karthik's direction, he thought of different possibilities and situations that could come and how he would react. He ensured that he was clean and presentable, so he took the most expensive facial package at a salon near his restaurant. Charlie was surprised with this new schedule of his boss as Krishna was always particular about his schedule. Charlie did not bother much as he got his instructions on time and guessed that Krishna was collaborating with Vivek for another restaurant. Krishna practiced on how to start introducing himself, how to approach and how to please his customers; he watched different genres of pornography to get a better idea of different poses and expectations. It was a Wednesday evening and Karthik's message had come with the details of Krishna's second customer.

"Hello Sripriya madam, I got your number from Karthik. What time do you want me to come?", said Krishna nonchalantly. "Around 730 in the evening, that's when my husband leaves for his night shift", came the reply in a hushed tone. Krishna parked his Bullet a couple of houses away and waited for five minutes before entering the house. He ensured that he was casual with no queerness in his gait. He wore his bag over his shoulders and the security of the apartment stopped him. He became nervous and told the apartment number. The security asked him the purpose but Krishna was not prepared. At the spur of the moment he replied he came to deliver a parcel. The security asked him to show the parcel and Krishna was getting irritated and tensed. He didn't know what to answer; slowly took out a brown colour paper cover from his bag and the security let him go. Krishna thanked the pharmacist who kept the condom inside the paper cover instead of handing over the box to him directly.

When Sripriya opened the door, he observed that all lights inside the house were turned off and only the night lamp was on. He could see that she was wearing a nightgown, around 30, dark skinned, fat and around 5'5" in height. He told her to pay and as she handed over the cash she asked him hesitantly, "I want you to start by licking here", pointing towards her vagina. Krishna was unprepared as Karthik also didn't inform him about this. Krishna obliged and both went to the bedroom.

They removed their clothes, he knelt down and as he started licking it became wet. He did not want to continue as two strands of pubic hair was in his mouth. As both moved towards the bed, she tried kissing him, but he pushed her away as his mouth was irritating him because of the hair. He didn't have time to ask for a tissue so licked the hair strands off his hand. Then both had a magical time for the next few seconds.

Krishna cleaned up first and went to the hall and sat. Sripriya took some time to change and when she came into the hall she was surprised to see Krishna ready to leave as she expected to talk to him. Krishna said, "Madam you need to pay me another 300 for licking". She stared at him for a moment and took out money and gave it to him and asked, "do you want to have something?". The doorbell rang and she quickly ran to the main door and saw thru the keyhole, turned at Krishna, "shit, its my husband. Maybe he suspected, what do we do?", panicked Sripriya. Krishna immediately went to her, kept his hands on her shoulders and said, "relax". He shouted on top of his voice, "madam, looks like the fuse is gone." He took a faulty fuse from his bag and opened the door. Sripriya was awestruck at his speed and presence of mind. He told a rotund man in front of him, "sir, I am from the electricity board, I was on rounds and came to know about this issue here". He gave the faulty fuse to the rotund man and without looking back he left. As he left, he smiled to himself on the confidence he had in asking her more money, the confidence he had in handling an emergency and he knew he was slowly getting into the game.

Krishna spent his time reading articles on how this escort service works, the possible diseases that could be contracted because of sexual activities and different ways to impress women in bed. He purchased two expensive vibrators, a few special underwears which cover only the crotch and has large openings on the rear which exposed the butt, some stickers that could pasted on the nipples; and got all these shipped from the USA. He also came up with a unique idea to paste some wet wipes with a tape on his thigh so that if he had to lick then he could immediately use to wipe off his tongue. He ensured he had an extra pair of clothes and underwear in his bag always. In addition to the vodka bottle, he kept water, some tetra pack juices and small black covers to throw off his condoms. As he started getting more leads, he was improvising more.

Krishna's third customer, Kanaka, was a receptionist at a hotel and had a troublesome marriage. She was in her mid-20s, dark skinned and was around 5'2" in height. She wanted to be on top of him. As she bounced on him up and down he realized that this needed more energy than the regular man on top. So he decided to charge accordingly. He planned to keep his bike away from the destination, at least four or five houses away. He did a recce wherever possible. Kanaka house was a stone's throw away from the Chetpet police station. So he had to park his bike in the next street and walk all the way to her house. He had to ensure that he was not recorded on the CCTV wherever possible and hence started wearing a cap wherever he went. He knew that the same cap would be an easy recognizable accessory and so bought five caps. He took different routes while reaching and leaving from a place even though it was a detour. With every customer, he kept improvising. By now he knew the routine workarounds that could be done, standard answers to the questions from the security, writing incorrect mobile numbers in the entry register and taking stairs instead of elevators as there is less risk of CCTV.

"Can you come at three in the afternoon tomorrow?", said Sridevi, Krishna's fourth customer. She was staying in the 6th floor in an apartment complex in Porur. He was surprised to see an old man, around late 70s open the door when he rang the bell. He just stepped back for a moment to check if he knocked the right door or not. As he was reconfirming the door number with the message on his phone, Sridevi said, "please come in". She was in her early 30s, around 5'6" in height, thin and wheatish. She was wearing a three-forth blue nightgown and her legs were completely waxed unlike his previous customers. He guessed it was her father, "he's my father-in-law, he's deaf. Please sit, give me five minutes; and ya, don't think much about how he opened the door", smiled Sridevi as she walked into the kitchen. Her father-in-law gestured to Krishna to sit next to him. With his wide smile he asked for water, coffee and food, and Krishna kept denying. "Why did you come?", asked Sridevi's father-in-law. Krishna did not know what to tell and just as he was about to open his mouth, "he's the new yoga teacher", shouted Sridevi as she came with a tray with three cups and offered coffee to Krishna and her father-in-law.

Krishna denied but her father-in-law insisted. She went to his left ear and shouted, "he's the new yoga teacher". Her father-in-law shouted back, "What? In the last two months you have changed three yoga teachers?". Krishna just started sipping his coffee and as he heard him, spurted out the coffee. Sridevi started laughing and went to the kitchen to get some tissues. "What happened? Are you ok? Coffee is not hot. Why did you spurt? Sridevi, please get some water to this teacher", told her father-in-law as Krishna could not stop coughing and indicated to him that he was alright. Krishna calmed down and started to take another sip, "By the way, are you certified? How many people have you trained?", asked the old man calmly. Krishna was careful this time not to spurt and knew that this was a wrong time to continue with the coffee and kept the cup down. "I don't know what went wrong. The last two teachers were there only for five minutes and left. Please be with her for at least 30 minutes. I will not disturb you two", said the father-in-law and started to walk inside his room. She indicated to him to come inside her room and closed all curtains but one, just to barely let light inside. She closed the door and instructed him to remove his clothes. As she observed his special transparent plastic underwear she got excited and came close to him and held his testicles. "Oh my god, your underwear is turning me on," giggled Sridevi as she removed her nightgown. She pointed to the oil and said, "I didn't try this with the other two before. So lets see how good are you at massage". After a thorough oil massage, both moaned loudly and it didn't make much difference to her father-in-law as he was watching some songs on the television in the next room. She told him to clean up, put on her nightgown and went to the kitchen.

By the time he came back her father-in-law was in the sofa in the hall and was eating noodles. He gestured to Krishna to sit down and requested him to have the noodles. He was very hesitant and he heard Sridevi as she entered the hall from the kitchen with her plate, "I had a really good time, you were very gentle. Please have some noodles. I also brought some more coffee". Krishna put up a fake smile in front of her father-in-law and hesitantly picked up the fork to have a bite, "I told you at least thirty minutes but you came out in twenty". Krishna didn't know whether to continue eating or stop to answer him. Sridevi moved towards her father-in-law and shouted in his ear, "he will come back next week for a longer session", turned her head towards Krishna and said, "so Krishna, how about next Friday at 4pm". Krishna smiled and nodded his head. As he completed his noodles, Sridevi was meddling with her phone and having her noodles and her father-in-law was telling Krishna about a movie he saw yesterday. That's when he heard the bell ring and two bulbs glowed in the house. Sridevi opened the door and that's when Krishna figured out how her father-in-law opened the door despite being deaf. The maid servant came in and went to the balcony to do the dishes. Krishna completed his noodles and got up to leave. Krishna coughed, portrayed a fake smile and folded his hands to her father-in-law and turned to Sridevi and said, "Madam, you need to pay for the massage". "Will I not get a discount?", giggled Sridevi as she looked into the kitchen to see if her maid overheard her. He smiled and said, "Ok madam, it is 500, you please give me 300".

Krishna was not prepared for these requests of licking and massage as Karthik mentioned to him about only sex. He decided to charge for different services that were asked and pondered about what else he could offer. Just as he started writing down all the services that he could offer, he received a courier and was happy to see the items that he ordered. He was careful enough to hide it quickly inside his bag so that none of his staff could see. He thought about the services for about an hour and came up with this list with attractive names and brief description, like that of a new food menu from a unique cuisine at a star hotel.

Head Massage Mild head massage to set the mood. Duration: 10 minutes	200
Body Massage Full body massage with oil to stimulate the entire body. Duration: 20 minutes	500
Tasty treats Use of tongue on the vagina to enhance the mood. Duration: 1 minute	800
Tasty treats 2 Use of tongue on the butt hole for a unique experience. Duration: 1 minute	1000
Once Ecstasy Insertion of the penis into the vagina till the climax. Duration: as per process	3000
The Woman Leader Woman on top position. Duration: as per process	3500

Double The Trouble Insertion of the penis into the vagina for the second time till the climax. Duration: as per process	5000
VIP Entry Insertion of the penis into the butt hole for a mind-blowing experience. Duration: 1 minute	4000
Self-Appraisal Self-gratification. Duration: as per ejaculation (maximum of two times per session)	300
Vibration Usage of battery operated machine on the vagina and butt hole as per requirement: Duration: upto 3 minutes	500
El Chombo Strip dance with seductive moves, provocative underwear and nipple stickers. Duration: 3 minutes	500

Terms & conditions:

No homosexuality

No BDSM / multi-some

No handcuff or other restraints

All services are not comprehensive and can be revised on an as-and-when-required basis.

Krishna mentally prepared this rate card and saved the image on his mobile. He never shared the rate card with anyone of his customers as this was his unique selling proposition. In order to bring about a uniqueness in the service he was providing, he thought that he had to be different. As he was an observant individual, he figured out whom to read out the services roster. To some customers he would not tell anything, whereas to some customers he would tell them the services only partially as he knew that they would not understand what he is trying to tell.

Krishna continued his gym routine rigorously. He ensured that he was fit and well maintained, clean shaven and wore ironed clothes whenever he visited his customers. He ensured that he would spend as little time on personal talk and avoided as many questions as possible. He also ensured that he wouldn't ask any questions unless necessary or unless he felt it was needed. Something told his heart that in Jayapradha's case that she needed help and so suggested for a solution in her marital life; and more so since she was his first customer. He was thinking about her and wanted to help her out. He called her and she shouted over the call, "hi Krishna, how are you? I never expected you would call back". "I am fine madam, how are you? How is your schooling coming along?", replied Krishna. "Hey Krishna, all is well. Actually I was about to call you. Listen I have been tracking my husband and his activities over the last one month and I think your guess is correct. Give me a few more days so that I get more data. I just need to catch him red handed and need your help for help for that. Listen I have to go now, sorry again, but next time I will call". Just as the call got disconnected he got another call, "hi, this is Kushboo.

I got your number from Karthik". Krishna could hardly hear the voice on the other side, "Can you please speak a little louder? I can barely hear you", told Krishna. "Please come tomorrow at seven in the evening, get a big bottle of vodka, mango juice, two cigarette packets, two marijuana joints, one chicken lollipop, one mutton biriyani and one fish fry. Don't come by the stairs, there will be rope hanging, please use that to climb up", the voice was barely audible and the line got cut before he could tell anything. Krishna smiled at himself, thinking of the order list as this was the first time someone asked for food & marijuana and to top it all, rope. The last he had marijuana was with Abhinaya at the house. He figured out that he would be staying back at this customer's place, so packed himself an extra pair of clothes.

Krishna was curious who this customer was and did his recce. It was a plush apartment in T.Nagar and barely three or four houses. There were five cars parked and three of them were premium vehicles costing nothing less than forty lac rupees. He was wondering where the rope is and could not see it. He waited for a moment and lit a cigarette when the sixth car, the most expensive of all just entered. There were two men in the car, one elderly person and the other seemed to be his son, both were wearing white. It was evident that they had big businesses, else how could they maintain this lifestyle. He didn't bother much, completed his cigarette and left. The next day other than his restaurant work, he had to meet the doctor again for his stomach pain as it had resurfaced. Though it was mild, he didn't want to avoid it. He met a few of his cousins, spoke to Abhinaya after a long time as she was busy with her consulting assignments and in the evening got ready to meet his rich customer. He got all food from his restaurant, arranged for the marijuana, prepared the joint, bought the vodka and cigarettes; and wondered if the rope would be there and how he would climb with this bag. He reached early and was waiting for the right moment to enter. As the security and another person went upstairs, he sneaked in and went to the back. He did find the rope which was not there yesterday and got convinced that it was not a sham. The rope was tied to the balcony, and he started climbing. He looked on all sides and was convinced that he would not be noticed as there was an ongoing construction on both the sides. Though he used the support of the wall it was very challenging, he thanked the gym for the extra muscular power he developed in the last few months.

As he reached the balcony he could see the bedroom which was as big as his hall, marble-floored, a really thick mattress, a large-sized television and the room was heavily interior-designed. The bedroom door was open and he saw two women in early 20s wearing a red saree and the edge of the saree pulled over on their heads and they were seated on the floor. The two men he saw yesterday were still wearing white, seated on the sofa along with another man and an elderly woman. Both the women on the floor were wearing enough jewelry as if they were ready to attend a wedding. He saw another woman in early 20s walk past them and sit on the sofa, but she was wearing a black skirt and a blue blouse. He guessed that she would be his twentieth customer. He could barely hear anything but given his observation he was sure that there was a big argument going on. The elderly man was yelling at the other young man and the elderly woman placed her hand on her head. The woman on the floor started talking, then the elderly man got up and wanted to slap her but the girl in the skirt caught hold of him and made him sit. She stood next to this woman who was about to talk and indicated to apologize. The drama unfolded for another thirty minutes. All got up, the two women in saree touched the feet of all the people and moved towards the main door. After a moment, Krishna expected the black skirt girl to come but was surprised to find the woman who was about to revolt came into the bedroom; closed the door and ran towards the balcony where he was sitting. She opened the door, saw Krishna for a moment and confirmed to see if all had left. She indicated to him to come inside, apologized profusely, and closed the balcony door and all the curtains and wailed at the top of her voice. She took a stick from below the bed and started beating the bean bag vigorously as she swore every bad word he knew in his dictionary. Krishna didn't move a bit for the next two minutes. After she calmed down, she went to the bathroom and came out in just a camisole and shorts.

Kushboo came close to him, sat on the floor and said, "Lets have marijuana and just keep talking something". Krishna lit one and figured out that it was her first time, explained to her how to suck in the smoke completely inside, pause for a moment and then let the smoke out. She didn't speak the whole time but Krishna explained the different nuances of marijuana and his marijuana time in college. Just as they completed she came close to him and kissed him. He didn't try stopping her. She was fast and immediately removed his clothes and hers too, taking complete lead. She clung on to him as if she was climbing a tree, he lifted her as they continued kissing and then both fell on the bed and had sex. As he lied down next to her, she started crying and he told her, "can you please teach me how to cry at the drop of the hat?". She smiled, stopped crying, wore her clothes and threw his clothes at him, and told him to make the drinks. Both sat and without the traditional cheers, she gulped the first drink. He asked her, "first time?". She indicated to the cigarettes, lit one for herself, recollected the way to smoke marijuana and enjoyed her smoke. She again indicated to him for food, popped in a chicken lollipop and came close to him and gulped his drink as well and winked, "all of this is first time except the sex part".

Krishna made another drink for both, this time he raised the glass towards her and said, "cheers". In the meantime she finished her cigarette, lit another one and gulped her drink again. He didn't tell anything but understood that she was in tremendous pain and mentally drained. "Do you know how it feels to be chocked? I mean literally. What if I try to strangle you and warn you not to tell anyone?", said Kushboo nonchalantly. Krishna knew by now that he should not open his mouth. "My husband and I had an awesome honeymoon in Iceland. It was my first trip abroad and we saw the northern lights. It was the best thing that I saw in my life. I thanked my parents that I got married to a rich loving guy but all hell broke loose when we came back. He told me that I had to sit on the floor in front of his parents, wear saree covering my head, sit at home and cook meal three times a day. I fought with him badly and he started complaining to his parents. I knew that I had to adjust but not this bad. They started yelling at me everyday that I don't respect them. I have to get up everyday and touch their feet and the same routine before hitting the bed. I feel like pulling their legs when I do that", said Kushboo as she completed her cigarette.

She lit another one and continued, "Fights became bigger everyday. I couldn't open my mouth in front of them. My bastard husband never supported me and in the end yesterday he held me by my throat and threatened me not to raise my voice ever against him or his parents", she had tears as she told that, came towards Krishna, took his drink and gulped it. "That bitch sister of his has got married into a family where she drinks with her father-in-law, she can wear whatever she wants to and these bastards have no problem in seeing their daughter in shorts but the daughter-in-laws have to be covered head to toe. No looking into the eye, no going to parents house often, no adjustment in food as they need a full fucking seven-course meal both times in the day, no maid servants for an extra hand while cooking as these bastards think the maid cooks meat at her place and it is against their ethics, no dishwasher as they feel it wont wash well, well how many NOs. I can keep going on and on. My bastard husband wants to rest on Sunday and I end up in the kitchen for all days in the week. Yesterday after he held me by my throat, I poured out to my parents, everything that happened for the last six months for the first time. I don't know whats wrong with them. They disconnected the phone so coolly within two minutes saying this is the story in every house and I have to adjust. In every house does the husband choke the wife? What kind of fucking mindsets do my parents have and whats wrong with the girls' parents in this country? Do you know how much I had to plan for this – tell the maid to come in the afternoon tomorrow, ensure that I find out from my friends who is getting married, talk to them and make them talk to my husband, put an act such that a stranger whom I don't know is the best friend of mine who is getting married and to top it all promise to send a photo of me in the wedding". Krishna finished his drink and a cigarette.

She told Krishna to light another marijuana and make more drinks and while she was venting out, she completed the chicken lollipops and the fish fry. He said, "Madam, this will become too much and you are going too fast". "Just shut up and let me vent out", said Kushboo calmly and took the joint from Krishna. They both shared the joint and completed it slowly and both didn't utter a word. Both clinked their glasses and Kushboo continued, "I have always been a good painter and have a good sense of colours and shades. I wanted to continue with my studies in interior design but my parents told me that this is a prospective alliance as these bastards owned a jewelry store. I was also lured by their wealth and gave my nod. I was just about to start on my own and open an office. As a matter of fact my prospective clients even called me after I got married. I tried helping them out but couldn't do much. You know what I am numismatist as well. You should check out my collection, whereas this bastard husband of mine has barely seen it". As Kushboo got up excitedly to show her collections, she almost fell down and Krishna caught her. She tried to stabilize herself, walked slowly towards her cupboard and got the coin book. Krishna was amazed at the collection as he had not seen anything like this before. He was surprised to find that she had all the Indian coins post-independence. She explained all the coins, their intricacies, the mints where they are made and the coin exhibitions she attended. Both completed their glasses and Krishna got up to make more drinks. As he turned he saw tears rolling down Kushboo's face. She was lost in thought as she turned the pages of the coin book. He came towards her and handed her glass to her. She finished her drink in one gulp again and looked at Krishna nonchalantly and said, "I don't know what to do Krishna. Please help me here", and kissed him. Both were completely intoxicated in marijuana, alcohol & nicotine and kissed each other passionately for a long time, as they removed their clothes. Both enjoyed their best for the second time. Just as they climaxed Kushboo vomited everything that she ate and drank.

She was knocked out completely. Krishna got scared and checked her pulse and breath. Her pulse was fine. He helped her in the shower while she kept repeating the words continuously, "Krishna I don't know what to do. Please help me". After giving her head bath, he dried her hair, helped her with her cloths, and put her to sleep on the sofa in the hall. He changed the bedsheet and put the used one in the washing machine. He went to the hall to call her, but she vomited in hall as well. He changed her clothes again and put her to sleep on her bed. He turned on the TV in the hall and started having his dinner. He browsed thru the house; television so big which he had never seen in his life, house was completely air conditioned, kitchen had a double door refrigerator, all the bedrooms had a television and all the cupboards had an automatic light that glows when the door opens. He completed the mutton biriyani and slept on the sofa. This was the first time Krishna drank so much at his customers' place, first time that he stayed over and the second time he was getting personal. He felt very guilty and slept on sofa.

It was 10 in the morning when Krishna got up and went to the room to check on Kushboo. She was moving in the bed and was about to get up. He sat next to her and called her out. She got up holding her head and said, "I am having the worst headache that I have ever had". "This is called hangover", replied Krishna, got up and said, "shall I make some coffee?". She insisted that she would make and went to the kitchen and got some coffee. As both sat down in the hall, Krishna smiled and said, "do you remember what happened yesterday other that the sex piece?" Kushboo smiled and replied, "How much did we drink?" "We completed almost a full bottle of vodka, two packets of cigarettes and few joints. You vomited twice and I helped you with the bath twice. I spent one hour cleaning the bed and the room, and look in the balcony, your clothes and the bedsheet are getting dried. And one more thing, I don't want to embarrass you but you can check my phone if you want, I have not taken photos of you when you were asleep", replied Krishna without missing any detail. Kushboo was shocked to hear and kept her mouth open as she listened, but her head was paining badly and as she held her head, she said in a serious tone, "Krishna, you came into the house climbing the rope, you got everything that I asked for, and you patiently heard everything without judging me and let me vent out. As a matter of fact I wouldn't be surprised if you hadn't come yesterday given the fact that you had to use the rope to come up. I was anyway planning to get my own bottle and cigarettes if you had not come. So I trust whatever you say".

Krishna replied, "See Kushboo, listen to me. I am no one to you and the same applies to me. You told me to help you almost twenty five times last night. I thought about it in the night and the only solution I see is you have to divorce your husband and move on".. Kushboo's eyes became wide open and she stopped sipping her coffee. She shouted at him, "What the hell are you telling? How can you say that? Do you even know what you are talking?". Krishna replied calmly, "see Kushboo, please hear me out completely without interrupting me, then you decide whatever you want to decide. From whatever you told me and whatever I observed, you are someone who is actually good at interior designing and if given a choice you will take it up as a profession. You have a great interest in numismatics whereas your husband doesn't even cares about it. Do you know whats today date? Its 15th August 2019. We are celebrating our 72nd independence day and unfortunately you are still not free. You are showing your frustrations to your husband but he also doesn't cares about this because he has seen women around him all his life like this and so he thinks this is normal. Imagine you are made to sit on the floor when the other person in front of you is sitting on the sofa which is basically indicating you to be a slave in front of the other person. You are completely shackled, both physically and mentally. You are trying to break these shackles but unfortunately even your parents are not supporting you. You give yourself a convincing answer to the question: can I sit on the floor everyday like this for the rest of my life? Can I keep covering my head with saree everyday for the rest of my life? Can I keep getting chocked by my husband occasionally? Given whatever you said, I am pretty sure that you have a double-digit number of missed calls since morning".

Kushboo checked her phone for the first time since morning and found thirteen missed calls from her husband and gave shocking expression to Krishna. "I mean come on. I am able to figure this out just by four hours of interaction with you and I am sure that you will not have convincing answers to the questions I asked. You are getting suffocated everyday, its like breathing thru an oxygen mask every moment. You got angry when I uttered the word divorce, but then at the same time how can you blame or get angry with your parents about their mindset. You have to blame yourself for your mindset right: you got lured by the wealth and got married, you are not able to make a strong choice for yourself and you are being a hypocrite by telling you are fine but your parents are at fault. I am sorry if I am entering into your personal space but if you feel that whatever I have told you doesn't make sense then fine, it is your choice", ended Krishna with a serious tone.

Tears rolled down Kushboo's cheeks. Krishna was calm and continued sipping his coffee. The bell rang and Kushboo became panicked and ran towards the main door and came back screaming in fear, "oh shit, its my husband's aunt who stays in the next house, what do I do?". Krishna kept his hands over her shoulder and calmly replied, "relax, please relax. I will handle the situation". He ran to the balcony, brought his slippers and placed it near the main door, sat on the sofa with his bag near him and indicated to Kushboo to open the door. "How much time do you take Kushboo?" asked a fat aunty in saree as she starred at Krishna and starred back to Kushboo and said loudly so that Krishna could hear, "just because you are alone it doesn't mean you can wear such clothes and how can you wear such clothes in front of strangers?"

Krishna replied, "hello aunty, I am Krishna. I am a sales representative for the door-to-door sales of a product which is good for back pain. It is battery operated and very effective. I just spoke to madam and she wanted to check the product for herself so called me inside". Kushboo was wondering what Krishna was telling and as Krishna was replying to the aunty he took out the vibrator from his bag and gave it to the aunty. Kushboo could not control her laughter. Krishna explained all the features of the vibrator and asked the aunty to test it on herself and she replied, "all ok but the shape looks very odd". Kushboo burst out laughing. "Madam there is nothing to laugh here, it is an effective product, why don't you try it for yourself?", told Krishna in a calm tone and winked at Kushboo. The aunty was confused as to why Kushboo was laughing and told Krishna, "so how much is this and more importantly how much discount will you offer?" Krishna replied, "as you can see the price tag says 6000 rupees, and I can give 5% discount". "I will not buy unless you give 15% discount", replied the aunty in a demanding tone. Kushboo tried hard to control her laughter and by then Krishna replied to the aunty, "if this madam also buys along with you aunty then I can give for 15% discount". Kushboo smiled and told, "aunty I have had the demo of this and it is very good. I am taking it". Krishna replied, "ok fine, I will come back tomorrow with two numbers and thanks to both of you for your order" and left.

Krishna continued his 'other activity' whenever possible but at times denied taking Karthik's requests for genuine reasons as he had to meet Vivek sometimes for other business opportunities. Sometimes he also had to meet Vivek's father to go thru the financials as his father was impressed at the way Krishna maintained his data. He even took some of Krishna's ideas and implemented in his other businesses. Abhinaya was busy in settling down with Abdul as both took an apartment in OMR. She met Krishna barely as her consulting assignments took most of her time. But whenever Abhinaya and Krishna met they ensured they spent a good quality time, their most favorite hangout being the beach. It was 11 in the night and they came for an ice-cream to the beach. Abhinaya enquired about his stomach pain, restaurant and prospective expansion in the near future. "Charlie was mentioning that your schedules have changed, what happened Krishna, any new found interest", giggled Abhinaya. Krishna smiled and replied, "if I come across someone special then I will surely let you know Abhinaya". Both started driving back home and Abhinaya was in her usual pose, closed her eyes and was pinching the skin between the eyes. "Please do settle down fast. The more time you spend in the initial years together, the better you will come to know of each other. The moment you have kids then your priorities for the kid will increase and the couple-time will reduce significantly", told Abhinaya in a serious tone. As they reached home, Krishna carried her like a rice bag on his back and didn't utter a word, he was lost in thought, "what did Charlie tell her, what does she know about my 'other activity', did she look into my bag when I was not near it, should I tell Abhinaya about my recent 'other activity' or not, actually she is right, I should settle down, I genuinely feel I should settle down, should I follow Karthik's style of getting settled down with one of the customers or find someone else, but what will happen when that someone else finds out. I am confused."

In the evening, Krishna was checking his files in the restaurant when he got a message from Jayapradha if he could meet her at a coffee shop. Krishna delegated some work to Charlie and left to meet her. Just as he reached the coffee shop, a burqa-clad woman came close to him and said, "Krishna, you are right on time. Come with me". Krishna was shocked and took a moment to realize that it was Jayapradha's voice. Both sat in a corner table and Jayapradha indicated to Krishna towards a table on the other corner. Her husband Ravi was with Ramarajan. Both were laughing as they spoke and Jayapradha whispered to him, "like I said, I have been following both for the last one month. I think we are just there. I need to catch them both in action. Once it was evening 10 and I could hear moaning sounds outside Ramarajan's door. You know what, that night Ravi didn't come home". Krishna was shocked to hear this and said loudly, "you were standing outside his door to hear them in action". Jayapradha put her finger on her lips and said, "I could have thumped his door that night but they could have taken their sweet time to open the door and cover up everything. Look Krishna the only way is there is a curtain next to the door. Even if the curtain is partially open I can create a scene when I see them, but how do I get a small peek into the house. Thankfully it is a studio apartment and so they have their time in the main room only. Please think of something Krishna".

Krishna listened to this quietly as he sipped his coffee. He could see anxiety in Jayapradha's eyes and was expecting an answer. Krishna replied, "I think we can do something about it if the curtain hooks are metallic, if it is plastic then maybe we will have to think of something else. Did you observe that?" Jayapradha thought hard and said in a puzzled tone, "shit, no. Krishna, now what should we do. Look they are leaving, I am sure they are going to that room now. We have to catch them now". Krishna gulped his coffee, paid and both left. As they were following Jayapradha's husband, she asked Krishna, "did you think of anything?" Krishna replied, "please relax, lets go and see first. Then decide whether we must barge into the room or think about it another day. I understand your point when you said thumping on the door, that will not work out and if that happens your husband will realize that you are following him, and everything will go for a toss". Ravi and his partner Ramarajan stopped at a building and went upstairs. Krishna and Jayapradha waited outside the building. Krishna told Jayapradha to wait for a minute. "What the hell are you doing? Why are you leaving me and going away?", screamed Jayapradha at Krishna. He replied calmly, "give me ten minutes. I saw an old paper shop nearby while coming, typically they will have magnets to remove iron metallic particles off the junk. I will request that person to borrow it for sometime. If the hooks are metallic then maybe we can use the magnet to slightly move the curtain by standing outside. Three things here: I hope he gives the magnet, I hope the hooks are metallic and most importantly I hope your husband and his partner are in action".

Jayapradha moved the veil away for this first time and was amazed with Krishna's reply, her eyes were wide open, showed both her thumbs to Krishna and winked at him. Krishna was back in eight minutes as Jayapradha was counting the time. As Krishna came back, he was surprised because she removed the burqa. Both went upstairs and were lucky to find curtains hooks to be metallic. He placed the magnet on the window frame and it worked, the curtain moved a little bit. Jayapradha whispered to him, "Don't worry, I will not faint by seeing them in action. I have mentally prepared my mind after seeing enough gay porn videos". Krishna smiled and replied, "Don't worry, this is nothing new. Homosexuality is in nature. Its not abnormal". After a few attempts, the curtain moved further and both saw Ravi and Ramarajan in just their underwear and kissing each other passionately. Jayapradha didn't wait for a second and screamed her husband's name at top of her voice. Ravi and Ramarajan were shocked when they looked at the window, their face became white with fear. Both scrambled for their clothes as Jayapradha screamed again. Krishna was conscious if someone would hear her but luckily no one came over. Ravi opened the door and pulled Jayapradha and Krishna inside and immediately closed the door. Ramarajan couldn't look anyone into the eyes, covered his face, sat in a corner and started crying. Ravi fell at his wife's feet and cried badly and told her not to shout. Jayapradha was filled with rage and shouted at him, "what the hell are you doing? How long has this been going on? I will immediately inform all of this to all your friends at work and will complaint to the police. What the hell about my life? Did you ever think about me". Ravi continued crying and folded his hands and asked her to calm down and again fell at her feet. Ramarajan fell at Krishna's feet and said, "sir, please ask her to calm down. I will explain, please tell her not to shout. I will explain everything". Krishna came close to Jayapradha and said, "I think you should relax Jayapradha, please hear them out".

Ravi admitted that he was gay and has been with Ramarajan for two years. He didn't have the courage to reveal to his father who was bed-ridden and so got married under pressure. He assumed that Jayapradha would get bored of him eventually and would move on but never ever suspected that he would get caught by her. Ramarajan on the other hand was getting pressurized to get married but couldn't face his parents either. Jayapradha heard their story completely and turned to Krishna and said angrily, "So what do want me to do with them? I think we should report this to the police. What do you say?" Krishna replied calmly as both of them started crying, pleading and apologized again, "She's my friend at her school and suspected you two and told me to help her out. What you have done Ravi, is completely unacceptable.

There is nothing wrong in being a homosexual, but you have cheated her by agreeing to marry her and start a family with her. You could have denied the marriage. She's not bothered about you being a homosexual but about you marrying her and cheating her. I suggest you, Ramarajan, please explain to your parents in detail about yourself and if needed take a doctor along with you. And Ravi you should initiate a divorce from your side and you should also inform her parents about your condition along with a doctor. With substantial information and a certified professional's support both of you should take these steps to have a peaceful future". Both agreed and Jayapradha seemed to have calmed down. Krishna came out, lighted a cigarette and waited near his bike. After sometime Jayapradha came down thanked Krishna profusely. "Cigarette?", asked Krishna. She replied, "I stopped smoking and you should too. I am at my parents place today and told him to meet me there tomorrow. I have indicated to my parents already so that it doesn't come as a shocker to them but let them hear from the horses' mouth. Krishna, I really really appreciate that you came immediately else we would have missed this moment. Thank you for coming into my life Krishna". Jayapradha had tears as she said the last line. Krishna felt that sense of accomplishment as he really made a mark in someone's life.

Chapter 4

RADHA

Krishna became busy with Vivek in one of the new business models in the food and catering industry, cloud kitchen. Due to the increasing demand of ordering food online and number of increasing IT professionals in the city this seemed to be a good investment opportunity. By using the existing brand, they became busy with the plan of opening a cloud kitchen on OMR. This time Vivek was spending more time with Krishna trying to understand the nitty-gritties of the business and trying to optimize the personnel needed as they could easily move between Adyar and OMR. They had a difficult time in trying to finalize the place and after looking at ten different places over three weeks, they zeroed in on one. It was a long time since Krishna had a burger and took Vivek to a local burger place. Just as they were entering Vivek got an urgent call from one of his customers and apologized to Krishna as he had to leave. Krishna decided to have his burger as his evening snack. As he entered he saw there were just two tables with customers. He was browsing thru the menu on the wall and decided to go with the Combo 7. He told, "Combo 7 veg panner burger with fries" and heard the same sequence of words in unison with his voice. He turned and saw a thin tall fair girl, as tall as him and both smiled at each other. Both the cashiers were surprised as they heard the same from both the customers at the same time. Krishna paid and sat in the corner so that he could see the counter. The girl waited for some more time, ordered a drink and sat in a table so that she could see him. Krishna put on his headphone and started watching his favorite show, Last Week Tonight. He didn't look at her but she looked late-20s and was browsing her phone. Her hair was straightened and colored in burgundy, and she was wearing a black T-shirt and black jeans. She wore wedges and carried a handbag. As he was observing her, she made an eye contact towards him, Krishna became conscious and continued watching the show. The waiter served both and Krishna enjoyed every bite of the burger.

He received a conference call from Charlie and Vivek, he was guiding both on the logistics required for the new place and while doing so dropped his bike keys. As he was guiding them, he observed that the keys fell in a corner and was difficult to reach so he bent completely and found them. Just as he got back up, he was surprised to see that girl sitting in front of him. His mouth was wide open and didn't reply to what Charlie and Vivek were asking. They started getting impatient with him and he replied, "ok listen I will call you back" and took off his headphones. "Radha", said Radha. He was still unable to believe that a beautiful girl walked up to him and sat with him. "Radha", said Radha questioningly. He said hesitantly, "sorry, Krishna, Krishna" and extended his hand. She didn't extend her hand to greet him with a handshake but picked up her burger and said, "your name is only Krishna or Krishna Krishna". Krishna took his hand back, smiled and said, "my name is Krishna and I am surprised that you came and sat here". He received the call again from Charlie and this time both Charlie and Vivek were angry with him. He indicated to Radha that he will be back and went out for almost ten minutes, most of the time trying to cool down Vivek and Charlie and at the same moment answering their queries on the logistics requirement. He came back and apologized again to Radha. "Actually I am new to Chennai and am from Pune, I work for an IT company and stay in OMR; so can tell me a few places to visit here over the weekend", asked Radha as she moved her hair over her left ear. Krishna tried hard not to look at that and only focus on her eyes and was still thinking in his mind, "why did she come to me, she could have asked this to anyone, is she stalking me, what is wrong with her". Krishna explained to her all the places that are near Chennai for a day visit and even a few that needed a stay. He gave brief descriptions for all the places, the time it would take to reach them, the amount of time needed to spend at each place, the best time to go and was also showing a few pictures from his phone. She heard everything patiently and told him, "it going to be sunset, can you please take me to the beach if it is ok with you. I have never been to a beach in my life".

Krishna couldn't believe the last words that he heard from Radha. He was thinking loudly, "how is it possible that one has never been to a beach, why is she asking me to take her, is she mentally fine or is she a bold girl who doesn't minds moving with strangers, do I avoid her or do I oblige to her". "See, if you have some other work that is fine, please let me know the directions so that I can drive", said Radha as she completed her drink. "Well actually

I have some pending work at the restaurant which I am planning to open shortly, but its ok, I am tired and need a break now. I can take you to the beach but I have to leave in two hours", replied Krishna very slowly. "Ok fine, thanks for your time, I really appreciate it. Lets go in my car. You can leave your bike here. I will drop you back here, I insist please", said Radha with a smile. Krishna nodded his head hesitantly and wondered how she knew about his bike. Krishna didn't talk anything but was guiding her and at the same time attending calls from Charlie who was seeking his guidance. As they reached the Thiruvanmiyur beach and started walking on the sand, Radha handed over her bag to Krishna and started walking fast towards the beach. He had to catch up to her speed and she entered the water. She played around for some time and got wet completely. She forced Krishna many times, but he denied as he was busy with his calls. He warned her not to go inside the water a couple of times, but she ignored him.

After around twenty minutes she sat down in the beach with waves lapping on her. She was lost in thought and didn't look at Krishna. He wanted to enquire if she was fine but didn't want to disturb her 'me-time'. It was getting late for Krishna's appointment with a customer as she asked him to come by nine in the night. He went to Radha and was shocked to find tears rolling down her face. "Thanks a lot for this Krishna. I never expected this from a stranger, you obliged without any hesitation. I know you are getting late. We can go". Krishna didn't utter a word and said, "are you ok? Is there anything that you".., Radha cut him short and said, "I am fine, I will have to be fine, I will have to accept this fast and move on. Lets go".

Both walked towards the car and she didn't utter a word, Krishna continued with his calls as she drove fast. When they reached the burger place she got down as Krishna walked towards the bike and said, "Krishna, I will never forget this evening. You stood by me at the time when I needed". Krishna repeated the same words with the same tone, "are you ok? Is there anything that you". Radha cut him short and said, "please give me your number. I understand you are trying to help me out. I will call you for help when needed". Both exchanged their numbers and left.

Krishna became busy with his restaurant work and barely had time for his other activity. Karthik also called him less as he was getting his paperwork in place to leave to Dubai. Krishna didn't have time to think about the evening with Radha and didn't expect any call from her. He was trying to revise his menu at the restaurant and tried different combinations of dishes that could be packed effectively. He tried new packaging ideas for liquids like customized glass bottles but failed as risk of breakage was high during delivery. It was a Wednesday afternoon and his restaurant was full with customers. His phone rang, "Hi Krishna, this is".., Krishna stopped the woman on the call abruptly as he was busy with his work and replied, "yes madam, please tell me". "Can we meet today evening at 8?" He immediately told the woman on the call to give the location and disconnected the call. Krishna got ready in the evening, checked his bag and ensured he didn't miss anything and left for the address. He reached the address and found it to be a star hotel and called the customer, "hi madam I have reached, which room number?" "Room?

First come to restaurant on the ground floor and why are you calling me madam again", came the reply. Krishna was puzzled and didn't understand who this customer was. As he walked to the restaurant he saw Radha in a long black skirt and a white blouse. He put his hand on his head, started walking towards her and thought to himself, "oh shit, I didn't save Radha's number. Why did I mention room? What will she think now? How do I handle the situation? Why didn't I ask the details over phone?".

Krishna smiled and sat down in the table. "Madam, room, what's wrong with you. I thought you were starting another restaurant right, I mean cloud kitchen, or are you starting a hotel"., giggled Radha. "Look I am sorry I didn't save your number and I honestly never thought about that evening in the beach much, so I never expected your call", told Krishna apologetically. "Krishna, like I said, you were there at the time when I needed. I didn't expect you to hold me or hug me or cry along with me. You were there with me for two hours and that's all matters. I get your point when you said you didn't expect my call, that's completely understandable. If I was in your place I would think the same. By the way, today's dinner is on me, so please feel free to order. So, do you take alcohol?", asked Radha shyly as she sipped some water and called the waiter. "Yes I do, but I don't drink and drive", replied Krishna as he sipped some water and browsed the menu. Both ordered for food, Krishna ordered for his favorite pineapple juice and Radha ordered for a strong beer and said calmly, "So are you not curious to know what went thru my mind the other day?". Krishna paused for a moment and didn't know what to tell. Obviously he didn't want to tell her that he thought she was a prospective customer of his; so took some time to think and said, "see its been almost two weeks since we met and I didn't call you. As a matter of fact I didn't save your number and I didn't know what to expect when I came here. The other way round, you assumed that I saved your number and I came for you. At the same time, on the other day you wanted me at the beach and not the other way round. As you may recollect I was busy with my calls so I had nothing to loose in terms of time. Sorry if I am being blunt but that's the fact. But as I said on the other day, if you need anything please do let me know. I know this city like the back of my hand. And yes, please do tell me, what made you so emotional the other day?". Radha heard everything calmly and tears started rolling down her cheeks. Krishna got worried, got up and moved close to her, handed over the napkin on the table to her. The waiter got his pineapple juice and her strong beer. "Look I am sorry, my intention is to not hurt you but please note that I am always there if you need any help here. I took out time the other day because I could afford to. I mean how long would it have taken for me to tell a no, the other day. All that I am saying is if I have the time I will definitely help you out. Even today, though I didn't save your number, I had time so I came over", Krishna managed the situation smartly.

Radha indicated to him to sit down, wiped her tears and started in a serious tone, "Krishna, I didn't cry for what you said. The other day when we met, I was missing my mother who passed away last month and just that afternoon I had a miserable fight with my fiancé and we broke up. We were about to get married last month and after my mother died due to accident the wedding got postponed briefly, god knows what happened to him, he changed his stance. The day we did the final ceremony of my mother at home he told me about his feelings for his ex-girlfriend. I got wild. I knew about his ex but he said he was never in touch with her. Later I dug up his phone records and found that he had been in touch with that bitch for three years. Can you image this bastard spoke to her for 5 hours at a stretch sitting in my house when I was at office? I was devastated. I shouted at him, pleaded at him, got angry at him, begged him, warned him, but in the end I got tired as he said I am not able to forget her. The last fight was miserable, we had a heated discussion for twenty minutes and that's it. Its been two weeks and neither of us called each other. Though I have my brother and cousins helping me, I am having a difficult time in returning my wedding wear and jewelry by coordinating from here. I am having a difficult time managing my emotions. I am having a difficult time at work with people judging me. They think the marriage broke because of me. Why the fuck that in this country only girls are at fault always?".

Radha couldn't control herself and banged the table hard. The sound was loud enough for a couple at a distant table to turn towards them. Krishna was listening calmly and by now got used to women venting out non-stop without a pause. The waiter came running and apologized for the delay in the food. She apologized to him, ordered for another beer and continued in the same serious tone, "The moment this drama unfolded I got this transfer to Chennai from Pune. I was confused whether to take this up or not as I was not prepared mentally. What if this bastard changed his mind and came back to me, what if everything fell in place and we got married, I could have stayed back at my comfort zone. Every weekend was so nice in Pune, especially at this time of the year when the monsoon is just getting over. There are many ghat roads and scenic drives around Pune. We used to go on the bike for long drives, it was fun getting wet in the rain. It is an excellent place for nature lovers. My fiancé and I had only 3 months of courtship period, but our chemistry really gelled well. My mother was very happy. I lost my father when I was young. My fiancé and I met each other in a trekking event. It was so easy to convince each other's parents. It was like a movie and everything fell in place. I don't know what happened. Krishna, why do guys cheat on girls like this? Why did this happen to me? What should I do Krishna, please help me". Radha's tone started seriously and slowly became calm and ended in a confused tone. She was lost in thought and tears rolled down her eyes. She completed half her glass by now and the food arrived. The waiter noticed Radha's tears and looked at Krishna, Krishna indicated to the waiter to serve. Krishna continued sipping his juice and wondered why every girl who shared her story with him ended up with 'help me'.

Radha didn't look at Krishna and started eating her food. Krishna didn't initiate any kind of conversation. Radha completed her drink and food. "I think I will order for another beer to keep me suppressed for some time. Do you want any dessert?", asked Radha nonchalantly. "Radha don't, you will have to drive and here in Chennai police are pretty vigilant on drunken driving and yes I will take the butterscotch ice-cream", said Krishna in a concerning tone. "You said you will help me right Krishna, so can you please help me get home today", winked Radha. Krishna smiled and nodded his head. "So tell me your story, if you have any story at all", giggled Radha. Krishna told Radha about his school friends, about meeting his cousins every year, about his restaurant and about his studies in the USA. Radha listened to him quietly and was amused when she saw photo of Krishna with cousins in one of the wedding. Radha told about her schooling days, her friendly fights with her brother and about special way in which her cousins and friends go to each other houses at twelve in the night on their birthdays. After about thirty minutes of exchange of conversations, the waiter brought the bill and handed it over to Krishna. Radha warned Krishna, "hey I told you the bill is on me. Why are you doing this?" Krishna smiled and replied, "Don't you want to meet again so that you can pay next time". "Don't you know that you are dropping me off at my place now and we are meeting on Saturday evening wherein you are going to pay", pat came the reply from Radha as she giggled. Krishna's smile grew wider as he handed over the bill to Radha.

As Krishna drove her car, he saw her eyes were closed throughout the drive and tears were rolling down her cheeks. Just as they reached her place, she said, "Thanks a lot Krishna, you stood by me when I needed someone to hear me out and it means a lot to me". Krishna didn't reply anything. He booked his cab and told Radha, "Like I said, if there is anything that you".., Radha cut him short and said, "I am grateful to you for your help. Let's meet on Saturday evening. Show me a new place. Guess your cab has come. Good night". As Krishna got into the cab he was lost in thought, "last time at the beach I had work so I didn't bother about that incident much, I am now used to women venting out their frustrations but why is it that this time I am feeling a little different. I have helped Vivek's father, Charlie and Jayapradha but I felt emotional during those times as well. There is nothing special this time so I should not think about this much. Or like Abhinaya said I should start thinking of settling down. Is Radha that girl? But what about my other activity that is ongoing? I think Radha's emotions are temporary as she is low now and she needs some moral support, so I guess after she comes out of this low phase she will move on, but I don't know. I am confused".

Saturday nights are typically busy at his restaurant, but his most trusted staff Charlie would manage if told in advance. He told Charlie well in advance so that he could prepare himself. Krishna got ready and reached the nightclub in Guindy around 7. Radha was sitting on a sofa in the corner, was wearing a red T-shirt and black jeans with red lipstick. She waved to him and as he sat, he smiled and said, "it was difficult to get my bike the next day as the manager had to get convinced that I didn't leave the bike on purpose, they had to check the CCTV footage to really come to a conclusion that I drove the car back". Radha was puzzled, "oh Krishna, I am so sorry, why didn't you tell me, I mean I could have spoken to the manager on phone". Krishna smiled and showed his thumb to her, and both started browsing the menu. "So, is my boyfriend going to order pineapple juice now?", came a loud voice from behind and Krishna recognized it was Abhinaya. He closed his eyes and put his hand on his head, she came from behind and put her hands around him and hugged him tight. Radha was surprised, her eyes grew wide open and was curious to know who this girl was as she kept hugging Krishna. Abhinaya kissed him on his cheek, giggled and said, "So Krishna, who is this babe? Didn't I satisfy you enough in bed that you are looking for a change?". Radha got angry, got up and shouted, "Krishna, what the hell?" and took her bag and started to leave. Krishna got up and frowned at Abhinaya, blocked Radha's way and said, "Radha, sorry, hold on. She's my sister, she's just kidding around. Remember I showed you her pictures the other day". Abhinaya shouted, "Krishna, what the hell? You are sharing our pictures with a stranger". Krishna came close to Abhinaya and whispered, "What the fuck is wrong with you? How many times have I told you not to embarrass me?" Abhinaya giggled and replied loudly, "Why didn't you come to the airport to pick me up?" Krishna put his hand on the forehead and told Radha, "Sorry Radha, she has this habit of playing around, really sorry for this situation". Abhinaya told Radha, "Hey babe, sorry, I was just trying to play with him". Radha smiled and said, "sorry I couldn't recognize you from the photos". Abhinaya kept both her hands on her cheeks, tilted her head and smiled, "Am I not photogenic?" Radha couldn't control her laughter and said, "of course you are. Why don't you join us?" Krishna heaved a big sigh of relief and told Abhinaya, "Sorry, I completely missed your message Abhinaya, so how come you came alone this time? Where's Abdul?" As all three sat down, Abhinaya said, "I have come with my office friends, Abdul is stuck with an assignment and its ok that you couldn't come to the airport, I managed with my friends who are sitting at the other end. So, whats up Krishna, please introduce me to your beautiful new friend, Radha", giggled Abhinaya. Krishna had a twinkle in his eyes as he looked into Abhinaya's eyes, continued looking at her, pulled her cheeks and said, "Radha, she's my best friend first and sister next. She's the one who inspires me everyday. And yes, she's the one with whom I smoked for the first time, with whom I drank for the first time and with whom I had marijuana for the first time". Abhinaya smiled, pulled Krishna's cheeks and said, "Don't you think there is decorum to introduce people?" The waiter had come to take the order. Abhinaya winked at Radha and said, "So Krishna, today you have pineapple juice so that Radha and I can binge, and you can drive us back. What do you say". Krishna smiled and replied, "Do you think I have a choice?" Radha and Abhinaya ordered for their drinks and Radha said in amazement, "I am surprised to see such a lovely relationship between you two, I have never seen a brother-sister like this, so candid with each other. I am not so candid with my brother". Krishna covered his mouth and moved towards Radha and said loudly so that Abhinaya could hear, "Just waiting for her to get married so that I can get rid of 55kg". Radha couldn't control her laughter as Abhinaya threw a tissue paper on Krishna.

The drinks came and Krishna told the story of how he met Radha, how she had a bad breakup and how they ended up meeting again. Abhinaya quietly heard everything and excused herself as she had to meet her friends briefly. Krishna told Radha about his child prodigy sister, her acid attack, her mother's death and how her father disowned her mother. Tears rolled off Radha's face and she said, "She's undergone so much but yet so lively". "That's why I said she inspires me everyday", came the reply from Krishna. Abhinaya shouted, "Krishna, what the hell. Why are you making my friend cry?" Radha quickly wiped her tears and said, "Lets dance", got up, gave her phone to Krishna, Abhinaya also gave her phone to him. Both the girls hit the dancefloor as Krishna sat on the sofa and watched both. Krishna got a call from Charlie and had to attend to an issue at the restaurant. He spoke to him for a long time and made calls to others for resolving the issue. The girls came and completed their drinks, ordered for more and went back to the dancefloor. Krishna continued his calls, ordered for food, and indicated to the girls to come. They asked him to join them but he denied and continued his calls. It became 11 and Krishna again indicated to them to come and eat. Both came and as they sat Krishna was shocked and asked Abhinaya, "you just met her today and you both spent more time with each other than the time Radha has spent time with me". Abhinaya giggled and said, "well what to do we started the topics from birth and just came till kindergarten and you stopped us". Radha couldn't control her laughter as Krishna put his hand on his head. All of them completed their dinner and Radha insisted that she paid the bill but eventually Abhinaya ended up paying as she giggled, "let my company handle it".

Krishna was quite throughout the drive back home as Radha was in the back seat and was checking her messages and Abhinaya was in her usual pose with her eyes closed and pinching the area between her eyes.

"Thank you so much to you Abhinaya, it was a great evening. I am unwinding after a long time", said Radha with a wide smile. Krishna was surprised and replied, "Thanks to Abhinaya, I mean, this girl here. You just met her today and I came for you skipping my busy schedule at the restaurant". "Of course she will thank me Krishna, its obvious because I had to leave my colleagues and join you guys", said Abhinaya with open hands and wide eyes. "Whats there for you, just have to attend a few calls and in the end Charlie does everything for you. He mentioned that you goofed up two times last week and he had to apologize to customers because of your mess. So please shut up and drive" Krishna was shocked and tried to cover up, "What are you doing, are you spying on me? This is not right. Abhinaya, how many times have I told you not to insult me in front of others. You have.", Abhinaya placed her finger on his lips and indicated him to drive and said, "Krishna, just shut up and drive. I have told Radha about your last week's incident, so don't open your mouth and focus on your driving". Krishna placed his hand on his head, smiled and said, "Damn it, I am not able to get one single chance to corner you". Abhinaya continued, "And what are you doing nowadays, Charlie tells that you keep going out sometimes without telling him and you don't tell me things as well. Are you trying to do something on your own? Krishna, any new found interest in your life that you are not telling", giggled Abhinaya and looked at Radha. Radha also had a wide smile and tried to tease Krishna, "Oh really, Krishna, I never thought you are that kind of a person. So why don't you tell us. If you feel uncomfortable telling me then tell Abhinaya because eventually she will tell me".

Krishna got conscious and started thinking fast on what to reply. He replied in a serious tone, "Hey look, there is nothing like that ok. In case there is someone in my life then you will be first person to know Abhinaya, and you very well know that". Abhinaya looked at Radha and asked, "so what is your next book about? By the way Krishna she already wrote a book and is looking out for ideas for the second one. In case you need ideas for your next book ask Krishna, he will give you something really weird", laughed out Abhinaya. Radha took a pause and said, "Well, I have a few ideas, but after looking at you two, I guess I should write about you two. I haven't seen a brother-sister combo so cool. I am not and cannot be so open with my brother".

They reached Radha's apartment and she invited both home but it was too late as Abhinaya had to meet her colleagues for breakfast the next morning. Abhinaya and Krishna drove back to their house. "I am writing to Abdul about you and Radha", said Abhinaya. Krishna replied immediately, "What are you writing? There's nothing to write. I told you, if there is someone you will.", Abhinaya cut him short and said in a serious tone, "Krishna, I will show you the message when the time is right", and continued with her usual pose; eyes closed and pinching the skin between her eyes. As they reached home, Krishna continued with the same routine, carried her like a rice bag on his back and didn't utter a word, he was lost in thought, "what is Charlie telling her about my schedules. Does Charlie know about my 'other activity'? Is there a way he got some clue. There is no way he could access my phone password. Am I giving him too much a leeway. Now what did she message Abdul. There is nothing between

Radha and me. I am just trying to help her with the city. I did help many people before, especially Jayapradha, who messaged me that her parents, husbands' partner's parents were shell-shocked. But now she has moved on and applied for divorce. I definitely feel good that I have genuinely helped someone. What did these two girls talk about on the dancefloor? Anyway, let me not think about this much. But do I tell Abhinaya about my 'other activity'. I am confused."

Chapter 5

MORE ENDEAVORS

Krishna was editing the layout of the new cloud kitchen when Charlie walked up to him and asked for leave for three weeks. Krishna's eyes went wide open and asked him, "Charlie, is everything all right back at home? Three weeks is too much. You know we are launching the cloud kitchen soon and I need you". Charlie replied nonchalantly, "Krishna, when was the last time I took such a long leave other than the single day official off every week? I need to take my kids for a vacation to their grandparents place in Trichy" Krishna knew he couldn't argue with Charlie and said in a sad tone, "ok Charlie, make it two weeks. Please come back by the month end". Charlie didn't say a word, paused for a moment and replied, "ok, I will back by the 1st week of December. Now don't beg with me again, otherwise I will have to call Abhinaya". This irritated Krishna but he replied calmly, "Charlie, how often does she call you or you call her? What are you telling her about my occasional absence?". Charlie smiled, winked at him and left.

Krishna was confused and started wondering if he knew about his 'other activity'. His phone rang and it was

Kushboo and she was screaming with excitement, "Hi Krishna, long time. How are you?" How is your restaurant work coming along?". Krishna replied calmly, "I am doing good madam. How are you?". She again continued excitedly, "With your advice I am free now. You know what it was dramatic. I planned everything to a tee. I took a house for rent and made it my office, registered my office and spoke to my potential customers that I am back into business. In the meantime, I spoke to a lawyer and kept the divorce papers ready; spoke to a women rights organization and had my videos ready. Videos about how my in-laws made me sit down and shouted at me if I disobeyed; how my husband would choke me in case I raised my voice against that bastard or his parents. One fine day, I told that bastard husband of mine that I had to go home for a week's stay. So, I packed all my stuff with all my jewelry and moved to the new office-cum-house. Then I made an official police complaint and sent the divorce papers to my bastard husband and a copy to my parents, and I switched off my phone. It took them four days to find me and in the meantime I completed two potential deals from my new office for interior design of a house and a hotel. After that there was a roller-coaster of emotions from threatening to coaxing, by all of them. I told all of them to fuck-off. Hey Krishna, are you listening". Krishna was awestruck. He laughed loudly and said, "oh my god Kushboo, I never thought you were so bold. Amazing. I am really happy for you". Krishna had tears as he said that and heard Kushboo tell, "ok Krishna, I will tell you the details later, I am getting a call from a third potential customer. Lets meetup".

As Krishna kept the call, he wiped his tears and his phone rang again. As he picked up, Charlie came up to him. Krishna heard on the phone, "Hi, this is Regina. I got your number from Karthik. I am..", Charlie interrupted him and said, "I told Abhinaya that I see you talking hush-hush on the phone and most of the times it a woman's voice on the other side". Krishna consciously covered his mouth and told on the phone without hearing anything, "please send me the location and time details madam". He disconnected the call, scorned at Charlie and said, "ok fine. Do whatever you want, but at least stick to your committed date and be back on time". Krishna received a thank you message from Kushboo and felt elated that he could again help someone talented like Kushboo who was in a wrong marriage, and he got another message from Regina to meet her in the evening.

Krishna got ready and went to an address in Perambur. As he knocked on the door, a dark skinned old woman, aging more than 60 with a small hunch, around 5'5", wearing a long skirt opened the door. He was shocked and smiled with difficulty, and said apologetically, "I am sorry madam, I think I got the wrong house". The lady smiled and said, "oh Krishna, we spoke in the evening. You are on time. I am Regina". Krishna couldn't believe what he heard but assured himself that it's the same voice he heard in the evening. He had no second doubts about it. Then he silently cursed Charlie as he interrupted him during the call. Regina came close to Krishna and placed her right hand on his left shoulder. She took a deep breath and had tears as she said, "Thanks for coming without judgement, please come in and sit", Regina turned away and walked towards the table. Krishna was thinking fast about which excuse to make so that he could leave from that place immediately but on the other hand there was another thought running inside him, 'I have chosen to do this and she is my customer. She's right, why should I judge her based on her appearance or age, why should I judge anyone for that matter. Let me see what exactly she wants'. Regina knew that Krishna was still standing at the door. She could see his reflection off a glass on her table. She took her tablet & a glass of water, and without looking back said in a soft and sad tone, "So you still want to come in or leave? Its your choice, I have still not paid you. As a matter of fact, I am waiting to hear from you, what you will tell because I never revealed my age over phone to the last three people who came. I revealed my age to you and you came. So you have prepared your mind before coming. Thanks for that. The last three people either insulted me, verbally abused me or made fun of me; so there is nothing new that I can hear from you. But since you have seen me now and observed my hunch, I could expect something similar". Regina still didn't turn to look at Krishna.

He took a long breath and replied after a long pause in a serious tone, "Madam, I am sorry that I didn't hear you fully in the afternoon as my hotel staff was interrupting me, I should have asked you the details. But it doesn't matter because I am doing a service and you are my customer. Yes, you are right, both of us can equally reject each other but I have decided to extend my service to you. Tell me madam, what do you want from me", As Krishna started reciting his roster, Regina turned towards him and had tears. He continued his roster as he started walking in, closed the door behind and came to the sofa and sat down. Just as he completed the roster, Regina burst into a big laughter and said, "Wow, I didn't know so many things existed, and I didn't understand most of what you said. Guess I am getting old faster. Please explain me what each one is. Coffee?" Krishna smiled and nodded his head.

Krishna observed the entire house. The house was spic and span, and everything was in place, just like Jayapradha's house. There were some photos of Regina and her husband on the wall. He walked towards them and observed that they were a loving couple. Many photos were taken across different tourist destinations across India and there were a few wedding photos which the couple attended. He didn't observe any photo with their child. There was a keyboard in the other corner of the room. He walked towards it and pressed the key but there was no sound. He pressed again and heard, "You have to turn the power on. Do you know how to play the keyboard?", asked Regina. Krishna shyly replied, "I am sorry madam, I didn't mean to" and sat back in the sofa along with Regina. She started, "I am 65 and I worked as a nurse in the railway hospital. I still go there every day for support. I have been married for 40 years. My husband passed away around three years ago in an accident. You see he was a very loving man and we both enjoyed each other's company a lot. You know, I had a gem of a husband. I couldn't conceive and there wasn't an iota of regret that he married me. I will never forget him for that. He supported me thru all the emotional turmoil that we went thru. We decided that we will go for an adoption. After raising the boy for a few years, we found that he was a kleptomaniac. We put our heart and soul into the kid. We consulted different doctors and psychiatrists but unfortunately his habit became worse. On the day he turned 18 he ran away from the house. We searched for him in all possible places and couldn't find him. After searching for him for five years both my husband and I gave up. I didn't want any memory of my son haunting me now after my husband passed away, that's why you see there is no photo of my son. My husband and I decided that we should spent a lot of time travelling as our time for each other is valuable. My husband was working in the administration department in the railways. After he used to be back from work, I used to make him coffee and he used to sing some songs for me and play the piano. I don't know anything about the piano but used to enjoy listening to him. I clean it every day as it reminds me of him and gives me some comfort. I have relatives and friends around who come home sometimes and I do drop into their house often. The last one year I have been feeling lonely, psychologically I think I am getting into a depression. All kinds of thoughts run inside me and as a matter of fact, I even contemplated suicide". Krishna didn't react when he heard this.

Now he got used to the monologue of women, he knew the exact time when to break his silence. "How long do I stay like this, how many more days of this loneliness, I can visit my friends and relatives around once a week or once a month but after that? The last three weeks were very bad, all my relatives were away for different reasons and there was no one around. Though I am in a supporting role at the hospital now, I come back by 5 and I have nothing else to do other than make dinner for myself. The weekends are even crazy, though I am not needed at the hospital I end up going just to kill my time. I feel scared about my future, and I really missed my husband badly. I just needed someone to be with me, not for sex. I just needed someone with whom I could talk to. I just needed someone with whom I could share my situation. I ended up calling a few numbers after searching on the net. The first guy who came made a mockery of me even before I could open my mouth, the second guy verbally abused me of how an old lady can think of sex and the third guy insulted me outright saying that I am abnormal and I should go to a mental hospital. What do I do Krishna? Please help me", ended Regina as tears rolled down her face.

Krishna knew that his turn had come to talk. Both finished the coffee. He took a deep breath and said, "Madam I need some time to think. In the meantime, do you want me to explain to you the roster that I mentioned," smiled Krishna. Regina smiled, wiped her tears and said, "you are smart, you know how to make others happy, physically and psychologically", she winked at him, and both laughed. Krishna explained each line on his roster and Regina was giggling all the way. She was shocked to hear certain things and was amused to hear certain explanations provided by Krishna. Krishna asked hesitantly, "when was the last time you saw pornography?" Regina thought for a moment and said, "I don't know, I don't remember, actually may be I never saw pornography in my life except for whatever scenes that come in the movies. Actually my husband and I shared a good sex life, I guess fate worked the other way for us with respect to offspring. So, show me your list of items with some examples". Krishna was amused with her reply and showed a few videos explaining some of his items on his roster. Regina patiently heard whatever Krishna said and showed interest in a few videos. She even went back and forth on certain videos to understand the details. In the end Krishna asked, "so madam what do you want me to?". She pulled his cheek, had tears and said, "Krishna, I genuinely thank you for coming. That's all I wanted. Just lie down on the bed next to me this night and nothing else. I would like to feel the warmth of my husband thru you. That's it and nothing else". Regina couldn't control her tears and Krishna replied, "all girls are capable of crying at the drop of a hat, can you please teach me how do you do that?" Regina had a wide smile as she stopped crying, pulled his cheeks hard and he complained about the pain; she came close to him and said, "you really know how to keep people happy Krishna". Regina got up and said, "I have made dinner, mutton biriyani and fish curry. Do you take meat?" Krishna showed his right thumb. "By the way, would you like to try some home made wine that I made?" Krishna smiled and showed both his thumbs.

Regina got some wine and poured in two big wine glasses. They started having their drinks and Regina explained about her nursing work, her interesting experiences and depressing experiences at work and her trips with her husband. Krishna was hearing everything and trying to process her personality type. It became 12 in the night by the time they completed the entire bottle. After that Regina asked about Krishna and her restaurant. Krishna explained about his new business model and Regina was surprised to hear that there is this new concept. He liked the fish curry and asked for the recipe for his restaurant. After dinner, both went to the bedroom and lied down. Regina hugged him and put her left hand and left leg over him and tears started rolling down her face. Krishna asked in a soft tone, "Do I remove my clothes?" Regina pinched his cheeks and smiled and said, "No, you need not. Just don't talk". Regina closed her eyes and before the clock moved for a minute she slept. Krishna browsed his phone and checked for messages. After some time, he tried to move her hand and leg away as he was feeling heavy, but she went into deep sleep. Krishna had no choice and didn't want to disturb her, so slept in the same pose.

When Krishna got up in the morning it was 8 and for a moment he didn't realize where he was. He finished his morning ablutions and sat in the hall. He could hear noises in the kitchen and heard, "Good morning, you sleep like a baby". Krishna replied loudly, "yes, I was very tired yesterday. Sorry I didn't realize you got up. Do you need some help in the kitchen?" Regina came out with some coffee. "I must leave in another one hour, they are planning to introduce a new process and they would like some feedback from all of us. So lets have some hot dosas". Krishna hesitantly said, "Madam, I think you are taking unnecessary efforts, so please...", Regina cut him short, "so please what? Just shut up and come. Anyway, I have to make food for myself. So there is nothing unnecessary here". As Krishna sat down with her, he asked questioningly, "have you thought about marrying again?" Regina almost spilled her coffee on hearing this and said loudly, "What? What are you talking?" Krishna said, "Just hear me out for a few minutes. From whatever I heard from you, you are someone who is just happy with people around, no vocations or no activities. You don't read much newspaper or spend time on the internet getting to know things. You traveled lots with you husband and so you are open to meeting different people. You are dedicated to your work but you don't involve much with your colleagues at a personal level. You don't seem to be involved in any activity of any sort, which is fine for a person who has a family around. But it doesn't works for you right, because what else do you do on a daily basis. You get up, make food for yourself, go to work and come back and make food and sleep. In case you have children or husband then your work at home also increases accordingly right. Since you have no hobbies, you are finding it difficult to engage your mind. So, you end up going to relatives houses every month. Yes, it does give you a break but at the same time you are right, you are finding it mentally draining to take yourself there every month. So given all this I feel you need a life partner now, technically you need not marry but you can even live-in together. Who checks on old live-in partners nowadays?"

Regina heard him patiently and both laughed when Krishna mentioned about live-in partners. "See my point is, I heard of a 'senior citizens only' place in Coimbatore where you could even find physical assistance. It is not technically an old age home but a society for oldies. You should think of something like that or find someone whom you like at work. The choice is yours. I am only trying to give you an option wherein you could re-live your life. Don't bother much about what society or relatives or friends think about you. None of these three will help you solve your problem. They will of course give you suggestions or direction, but you as an individual must implement them. And whats wrong with the idea on live-in when there is nothing wrong ethically or morally, at this age", ended Krishna with a wink. Regina heard everything quietly and didn't utter a word. Krishna finished his breakfast and coffee, washed his hands and checked his bag. As he was about to leave, Regina came to the door, hugged him, and said in a soft tone as tears rolled down her eyes, "Thank you genuinely Krishna. I am so grateful to you. I will definitely think about what you said. Please call me for any help you need anytime. By the way how much do I pay you as hugging is not part of your list". Krishna smiled and said, "Well, you are actually right. Thanks for the pointer. I will add hugging in my list and will let you know so that you can transfer me later". Regina pulled his cheeks and said, "I dont know how to repay you for this, you really know how to make people happy. You have a wonderful gift".

Krishna's workload increased as Charlie was not available. Radha wanted to catch up a couple of times but he denied. He gave her the details of the place of interest over phone so that she could explore on her own. He even denied a couple of his 'other activity' calls but there was one caller who called him twice. "Hello, this is Mumtaz. I called you yesterday. Karthik gave me your number", said a muffled tone. Krishna was surprised as no one called him twice and replied, "send me the time and location details Madam" and cut the call. Krishna was surprised that someone could call twice for this service as this was the first time. He went to Mumtaz's house on a Friday afternoon. As he knocked the door, a short fair rotund lady in a green saree opened the door. She smiled and asked Krishna to come in and offered coffee. As Krishna sat, he observed that it was the most unkempt house he had seen. The newspapers were disorderly stacked, and the slippers were thrown around. On top of the dining table, other than the cooking related kitchenware everything else was there; spectacles, books, cleaning brush and even a bedsheet. The fan blades looked like they were never cleaned since they moved into the house. On the wall were a few photographs of Mumtaz and her husband at different scenic spots, and a few group photos as well. "Shall I put one spoon or two spoons, sugar?", shouted Mumtaz from the kitchen and Krishna replied, "one". Mumtaz came with two steel tumblers of different sizes on a dining plate and said, "sorry, the cups and saucers are under wash". Krishna smiled and said, "so can we start. I will have coffee later". Mumtaz blushed and said, "I will go inside and call you. I have a request, I would like me on top of you". Krishna knew that it would be very difficult as she was heavy.

Krishna heard her voice and entered the bedroom. She wanted woman on top and as she started moving up and down on him, he had difficulty in breathing as her entire weight was bouncing on him. He tried pushing her away, but she was in a state of ecstasy. She bent over him and asked him to suck her breasts as she continued moving up-down on him. Just as Mumtaz was reaching her climax Krishna felt wet over his face, for a moment he thought it was her saliva and then it struck him that it was milk. It was a shocker for him and at that moment Mumtaz shifted her position a little bit and ended up sitting on his erected penis as it bent in the downward direction. Krishna screamed in pain and pushed Mumtaz away. She was shocked and came close to him and asked him if he was ok as Krishna held his crotch in pain. He asked her if there was ice and she asked him to take it from the fridge. He was in pain and limped towards the kitchen, as Mumtaz put on her nighty. Krishna opened the fridge and was in a shock. Half the fridge was occupied with spices and the other half of the fridge was completely disorganized. He opened the freezer, took some ice and was trying to find out which cloth he could use but found an old torn cloth with rust markings. He limped back to the room, took his pant and went back to the kitchen, put ice in his pant pockets and kept on his crotch. He was still in pain but that was the first relief since his erected penis went exactly in the opposite direction because of over 80kg of weight.

He slowly limped back to the bedroom and sat on the floor with his legs spread and pocket full of ice on his crotch. As he was taking deep breaths, Mumtaz walked up to him and asked if everything was ok and apologized. He indicated her to go and sit on the bed. He browsed the bedroom and found the fan blades were never cleaned, a few toys and spoons under the bed, a tea cup on the side of the bed, cleaning brush and books on the bed. He looked straight at Mumtaz and asked, "so, why did you call me?" This was the first time Krishna asked such a question to his client. Mumtaz started crying and said, "my husband is not interested in me at all, and I have been telling him that I want a second kid and he never bothers to think about it. He's been postponing for three months, and I am sick and tired of him. He takes me out to his friends place every month but never brings them home here. I get tired handling my son at home, but he expects me to cook something different every day. He keeps pushing me to learn something online, anything of my choice but I need some rest in the afternoon. You don't know how difficult it is to handle a child single handedly; but he has a problem if I lie down for some time. He comes late every day because of his work and never helps me at home. Otherwise, he is a great person, he takes me out often and he has a good social life. He hits the gym every day in the morning and goes to cycling with his other group of friends over the weekend. He tries new restaurants every month, never hesitates if I have to buy clothes or stuff for the house. He likes me getting dressed up in all types of clothing, only thing is I am not keen on it. As a matter fact, he wants to revamp the house but I am the one who is denying him".

Krishna's pain subsided and he wore his clothes and asked, "can I look around the house?" Mumtaz acknowledged his request and wiped her tears. In the other bedroom a young boy was in deep sleep and just as Krishna opened the cupboard door, it creaked and the boy started crying. Mumtaz came running and took the boy into the first room. After a few minutes he came back and saw Mumtaz breast feeding the kid. She indicated to him to sit on the bed, but he denied and sat on the floor. Krishna said, "I know the solution to your problem and if you follow it your life be as you wished it to be". Mumtaz eyes went wide open and eagerly said, "oh really, please tell me. I was sexually frustrated and thus called you. Otherwise I really like my husband. I don't know what is wrong". Krishna cut her short and said in a serious tone, "everything is wrong with you Mumtaz. You are the culprit here".

Mumtaz was shocked to hear this and shouted, "what the hell are you telling?" Krishna said in a calm tone, "Hear me out for a few minutes and decide. You have given me coffee on a dining plate, you have kept honey in the fridge, you have kept curd in tea cup, half the masalas in the fridge have expired and there is a steel tumbler in the toilet acting as brush stand. When was the last time you ever cleaned the fans or arranged the newspapers or even checked what is underneath this bed or ever changed the newspapers in the cupboard, the last dated paper was 15.Aug.2015; come on, I mean you didn't find time to change the paper and clean the cupboard in the last four years. Whereas look at your husband, his clothes are organized, his cupboard is spic and span. He grooms himself very well, cares for his skin and hair. He hits the gym and is social. So how do you expect him to bring his friends to this decrepit house? If he is keeping himself up to date then he also expects the same from you, there is nothing wrong with that, that's why he likes you being seen in all types of clothing. He is interested in food and expects you to learn something online and cook for him. He is disciplined in his lifestyle and expects you to be the same. Three things Mumtaz: you are not grateful about the life you have, you are extremely lazy and you take your husband's effort for granted". Mumtaz had tears rolling down her face as she heard the last line and her son continued suckling on her. "So what to do you want me to do, Krishna? I get tired with my son. Please help me Krishna".

Krishna took a deep breath while thinking how many times he has heard the same sentence as the pain on his penis eased significantly. Mumtaz finished feeding her son and placed her next to him as he continued to sleep. He put on his clothes when she went to the bathroom to change and the kid started crying. She shouted to Krishna from the bathroom to lift him and hold him. As Krishna was lifting the kid keeping him close to his body, the kid vigorously kicked his legs and cried more. Since the kid was close to his body the kid kicked Krishna hard on his testicles. Krishna shrieked in pain as his earlier pain just subsided. He couldn't control this pain and fell on floor while holding the kid. Krishna laid down on the floor in pain and was cursing the kid as he stood next to Krishna's face. The crying grew louder and the kid urinated on his face. Mumtaz came out and was shocked to see her son urinating on Krishna. She couldn't control her laughter as she took the kid inside the bathroom. She gave her towel to Krishna to clean up. Mumtaz came out and apologized to him. Krishna went to the bathroom for cleaning up.

As he came out she giggled and said, "I am really sorry Krishna that my son pissed on you. Do you need anything else?" He smiled and replied, "That's fine. By the way, I will tell you what to do. I understand you are tired but lazing around will not help and as a matter of fact you need to loose a lot of weight to get to shape, which is healthy as well. Just take one cupboard or even half a cupboard everyday and clean it up completely. Keep a calendar for yourself, something like, I will clean the fans at the end of every month, I will clean the toilets on every Sunday morning; and stick to that schedule no matter what. Start seeing videos on how to organize the kitchen, how to loose weight and how to clean up the house. I guess you have never been to a parlor, so talk to your neighbors or friends and understand the basics before going and you will definitely need a complete makeover. My two cents, you will look wow if you straighten your hair". Mumtaz listened to everything patiently as she was trying to put her son to sleep and heard the door bell. She got panicked and said, "oh shit I think it's my husband, what do I do. He has come back early today as he is generally late on Fridays".

Krishna replied calmly and said, "just tell him I am deaf and dumb and I have come for a survey. I will handle the rest", and quickly went and sat in the sofa in the hall. As Mumtaz opened the door, Krishna saw a thin tall handsome male enter and Mumtaz told him the same lines which Krishna said. Krishna got up and smiled as he pulled a pad with a paper and pen on it. Krishna indicated with a sign language to him to fill a survey as Mumtaz's husband replied, "I can fill the survey but in this era who comes door-to-door for a survey when there are so many better online tools". Mumtaz became conscious and starred at Krishna as he calmly wrote a note telling that this is a small organization trying to make its mark by 'physically presence' and also help differently abled people. Mumtaz's husband filled the survey and as Krishna left he showed the thumb towards Mumtaz and left as he saw a teary sparkle in her eye.

It was a weekday afternoon and Krishna was a little relaxed as he sent his staff to the new place for the final checks. He was in a retrospective mode thinking about how he genuinely made an impact in people's life but at the same time another thought started coming to him on how long he would continue this 'other activity' of his as it was getting a bit monotonous. He recollected how only one customer so far opted for the 'Self-appraisal' option, wherein she stood nude in front of him and enjoyed seeing him masturbate as he sat on western commode in the toilet. For the first ejaculation he felt awkward as her eyes were on him and he had to put up a fake moan. At that moment he realized how easy and comfortable was ejaculation back at home. As he was just about to ejaculate, he held the shower handle so tightly that it broke. The second ejaculation was extremely tiring for him as it took more than ten minutes and she was getting impatient. He returned the money to her and removed it from his roster. There was another customer who asked for the 'VIP entry' and it was extremely painful for him and the customer. There was no way his penis would enter the butt hole.

One of the customer asked for 'Rim job' and that was first and last time he ever did that as it was his most bitter experience, literally and psychologically. He had five people ask for the 'Vibration' and seven of them for 'Tasty treats'. Most of them preferred him on top and only two of them asked for 'The woman leader' but after Mumtaz's experience he removed it from his roster. Only one customer asked for 'Double the trouble' and again that was his first and last. The second ejaculation took so long and the customer lost interest, his penis became hot and the vagina became impenetrable. Eight of them asked for head massage and four of them asked for body massage.

Five of his eleven in his roster were removed. Just as he was wondering how come no one asked opted for 'El Chombo', he received a call, "hi, I got your number from Karthik. This is Jayalakshmi. Can you please come over at 8 in the evening today?" Krishna took a long pause and acknowledged the request.

Krishna reached the address that was sent to him and just as he entered he saw the lights were dim. Even before he could fully enter the house, Jayalakshmi pulled him inside and quickly checked if anyone saw him and told him softly, "thanks a lot for coming, I am Jayalakshmi. Actually we are three people". Krishna immediately cut her short and said, "hey I don't do threesome, foursome. Please find someone else". Jayalakshmi became conscious and said, "ok, please listen to me for a minute. We are three best friends and two of us are holding a bachelorette party to our third friend who is getting married next week. No sex. We were actually looking for a stripper but where can we find such a service in India. Can you just entertain us?", winked Jayalakshmi as she indicated Krishna to sit.

Krishna had a wide smile as he heard that and was happy that at last he could provide the only service which no one has asked for, 'El Chombo'; which he had thought about just a few hours ago. He replied coolly, "ok fine, then I have the exact right thing for you. But I am pleasantly surprised that the culture of bachelorette parties started in India especially by calling a stripper. Good in a way that we are progressing in this front too". As he sat he saw two girls entering the hall. All the three girls giggled at each other and Jayalakshmi introduced Krishna to Jyotilakshmi and Jayamalini. Krishna eyes went wide open as he said, "are these your real names? Come on, I need to see your ID cards". All the girls burst into a big laughter as Jayalakshmi got up and said, "do you want something to drink? Can I get you some water?" Krishna grinned and said, "do you expect me to believe that there is nothing more than water at a bachelorette party, how about some white smoke, colourless smoke and coloured water?" Jayalakshmi winked and said, "well, we have actually completed two rounds of all. You are late".

Jayalakshmi played some music in a low volume, made drinks for all of them and started telling Krishna that they were working in a call centre, how they all met a couple of years ago and became the best of friends. She also informed that there was no issue of loud music as none of the neighbors had problem with sound but the only problem was men coming over. All of them completed their drinks and Jayalakshmi made another round and this time it was strong as Krishna wanted to begin the party on a high note. As they clinked their glasses again, Krishna got up and loudly said, "wish you a happy married life Jyotilakshmi, lets start the party", and gulped the entire glass in a few seconds. All the girls were in a shock as it was a strong one, Krishna started dancing to music and lit a cigarette, and the girls clapped to the tune. After a few songs and more dancing Jayalakshmi made another round of drink. The music and dance continued as all of them stepped in and the glasses became empty. Jayalakshmi got a joint, lit one and all of them passed it between themselves.

Krishna was quietly listening to their conversations as the girls made fun of each other. Jayalakshmi got up and made another drink. This time Krishna helped her and made another strong drink for himself and giggled as he put his arms around Jayalakshmi and said, "listen girls and listen you host Jayalakshmi, you are a bold girl and be the same way. Don't try to change this characteristic of yours as you are a fighter". Jayalakshmi hesitantly looked at the other two girls as she was not comfortable, Krishna came close to her and shouted, "so are you ready for the grand finale?". The music system started playing 'El Chombo'. He swayed his hips to the tunes and slowly removed his pants. All the girls hooted as Krishna stood showing his back to the girls. He wore a tight silk pink underwear wherein only his crotch was covered, and butt was revealing. The girls were in a shock as they looked at each other and gasped. Krishna turned towards them and made seductive moves while dancing to this song. All the girls giggled as the song continued. He changed songs to more racy numbers as the girls joined him in dancing. After five hours of partying, four packets of cigarettes, three joints and two bottles of vodka, it was one hell of a night.

It was around three in the night and Krishna requested the girls if he could sleep in the hall and he would go early in the morning. The next morning the moment Krishna got up he was surprised to see Jayalakshmi having breakfast and she indicated to him to join her and he said hesitantly, "look Jayalakshmi, I am sorry if I had overdone many things yesterday". She took a pause and replied, "well, yes, I became conscious when you put hands around me, more for the fact that you were drinking irresponsibly.

But that's ok, if you had crossed your limits I would have ensured that your pink underwear became red," winked Jayalakshmi. He smiled and said, "ok fine, I will leave now". She said in loud tone, "hello sir, I didn't make anything. This is left over fried chicken from yesterday. So please have and go", her tone changed now from seriousness to curiousness, "And what made you say whatever one liners you told about me. We were actually surprised that you got it spot on. They are still sleeping but I will definitely convey to them. So tell me, what made you tell that I am bold". Krishna scratched his head, got up, flossed him mouth and said while getting ready and checking his bag, "instincts, the moment you see a person you get an instinct. Science says that instincts or gut feeling is more for women than men. It kind of comes naturally to women. Well, for me I developed it over time. I am lucky that I got it right and in your case, I was confident the moment I saw you. See the point is, I feel you are someone who will put forth your point boldly even if it is not going to go well with many. How many people can do that with ease and without hesitation? Anyway, don't loose that trait of yours". There was a twinkle in Jayalakshmi's eyes as Krishna popped in some fried chicken. "Ok listen, I really have to leave now. With regard to the payment, well, you are the first customer to ask for this and may be probably the last. So consider it as my wedding gift to Jyotilakshmi", winked Krishna and left.

Chapter 6

THE PROPOSAL

Krishna met Vivek to finalize all the details and zero-in on a date for opening their cloud kitchen. Vivek was more than convinced with the details and they finalized with 15th December 2019. Krishna was happy and immediately called Charlie. Charlie congratulated him and said, "Krishna, you better start focusing now and spend more time now at the restaurant". Krishna replied in an irritated tone, "Please mind your business Charlie and lets get back to work". As he disconnected the phone he got another call and heard the sweetest voice he had ever heard, "Hi, is this Krishna? I got your number from Karthik. Can you come over in the afternoon around 3?" He took a moment, got up and moved away from Vivek and whispered to the woman, "ok, please send the location details". Vivek checked with him if everything was fine, he replied hesitatingly that everything was ok and became conscious if Vivek heard the conversation. Krishna reached the location on time and knocked the door. A thin tall fair bald girl in t-shirt and shorts opened the door and immediately pulled Krishna into the house and closed the door immediately. She indicated Krishna to sit on the bean bag and hurried to her laptop. She was smoking and had a vodka bottle next to her laptop with a drink made ready. She took a puff, sipped her drink, put on a wig, activated the camera on her laptop and continued with her call. Looking at what she did Krishna had a smile. She spoke some technicalities on software testing and the discussion continued for ten minutes. Every time she had to take a puff or a drink, she ensured that either she disconnected the video or hid herself.

Krishna smiled every time she did that and as the call got over she came to him while removing her wig and said apologetically folding her hands, "I am really really sorry Krishna. The call was supposed to get over at 3 and got extended by 20 minutes. It is irritating. Do you want to smoke or drink?" Krishna smiled and said, "yes, cigarette is fine". She lit a cigarette for herself and Krishna began to lean forward with the cigarette in his mouth to get it lit. "I am Satya. I work in an IT firm. I have lung cancer. Do you want to continue or you are free to leave?", said Satya in a nonchalant tone. Krishna moved back before the cigarette got lit, removed the cigarette from his mouth and took a moment to comprehend what Satya said because no one was so upfront with him. She turned away from him and said, "You are taking time, so I guess I know the answer. You can finish your cigarette and leave; or you can leave and finish your cigarette or you can do whatever the hell you want to. No problem. You are not the first. The first person left when he saw me bald. So I thought I should put on my wig for the second person but he left when he heard cancer. You are the third. Well, let me tell you this, cancer is not contagious and neither its like AIDS where you should be afraid that you will get it once we fuck",

Satya ended in an irritated and angry note while taking long puffs. Krishna kept the cigarette aside and looked at her and said, "I was not thinking about leaving, I was only thinking about you smoking when you actually have lung cancer". Satya turned towards him, smiled and said, "isn't is interesting, I started smoking after I came to know that I had lung cancer?" Krishna smiled, dictated his list and she asked him to start with a head massage which continued to a body massage and then ended up in sex.

Satya asked Krishna if he would like some coffee and he nodded. As Satya was preparing coffee, Krishna browsed thru the house. It was a single bedroom apartment with almost no furniture, just a mattress without bed, a bean bag and a cupboard. The bedroom had a work desk and a couple of chairs. He was wondering where the other furniture was when Satya said, "what else do you expect from a bachelorette's house?" Krishna became conscious that he got caught snooping and he replied, "sorry, I was just..", "looking around", Satya completed his sentence, winked at him, sat on the floor and said, "the best way to chat is to sit on the floor, don't you think so?" Both sat on the floor and started having their coffee. Krishna wanted to start the conversation and was hesitating, he kept looking around the house and continued sipping his coffee, he tried drinking his coffee fast but it was very hot. Satya on observing him smiled and said, "you want to know how I got cancer?" Krishna gasped at her and kept the cup down and said, "I,, sorry, I actually was,..", no words came out of his mouth when Satya emotionlessly said, "well, there is no reason for cancer right. It is said that in certain cases it is genetic and in certain cases it is lifestyle.

I had continuous back pain which I attributed to my work and neglected it for a while. I consulted an orthopedic and took an x-ray, everything was fine according to him, but the pain was cyclic. It used to be bad after the medications stopped but subsided during the medication. I changed two orthopedics but things remained the same. The third doctor was smart. He asked me if I had chest pain as well which I never figured it out and there was a mild doubt in the x-ray. Later after the CT scan, it was found that it was actually lung cancer which had spread to the spine and breasts. I was shell-shocked to hear this. My biggest wish in my life is to get married and it will not get fulfilled. The moment I told about my condition to my boss he told me I could permanently work from home as long as I could manage work. I am the only child and my parents don't know yet. I don't intend to tell my parents either. They are as such worried about me not getting married and I don't want to add this other news. I don't have cousins as there was only one of them and he passed away last year. The doctors told I have a few weeks left and need to start undergoing palliative care. The chemotherapy and radiation are just to prolong my days further. My only big dream since childhood was to have an understanding husband and a happy married life".

Satya gazed at her laptop while she sipped her coffee and had tears rolling down her cheeks. Krishna finished his coffee, went to the kitchen and kept his cup. He came back and said as he packed his bag, "Well, Satya I really don't know what to tell but in case you need any kind of assistance then please do let me know. I have only heard of cancer amongst friends' friends but haven't come across anyone personally, .so my best wishes to you. Just three things from my side and please don't deny: I run a restaurant with an Indian cuisine and you need anything specially made for you let me know. Don't put on a wig, just show your true self. Its not for people to feel bad for you but to kindle their humane portion of their mind. And thirdly, let me not accept any payment this time as you would need it for your treatment". Satya smiled as she wiped her tears, came to Krishna, hugged him and said, "Thanks for coming. Lets meet again with some yummy chicken biriyani then. Yes, you have a point, let me not put on a wig. And for the payment I don't want to argue now but I am not feeling good". Krishna winked at Satya as he was closing the door and said, "then keep a bigger bottle of vodka ready for Friday evening". As Krishna sat on his bike to leave, he was dull and felt bad for Satya, looked up at her apartment as he had tears in his eyes.

It was the Friday afternoon when Krishna informed Charlie that he would not be available in the evening. Charlie on hearing this got irritated and said, "Krishna I don't understand this. You know right we are opening another restaurant and it is just days away. And you been disappearing many times. I will have to take this up with Vivek sir". Krishna controlled his anger and replied sternly, "I am your boss, I run this place and Vivek is only a financier. And by the way, do you think he will care about your complaint". Charlie got more irritated and shouted at Krishna, "Fine, then let me talk to Abhinaya". Krishna knew that he was cornered. He had no choice but to listen to Charlie as he would inform Abhinaya about his absence and Abhinaya had a knack of figuring out Krishna's 'other activity'. He calmed down and put a fake smile at Charlie and said, "ok listen. I really need to meet someone this evening and I have to leave. Please manage today. I promise that I will handle everything over the weekend at both the locations. You can even take off this weekend along with your Monday off. You get a long weekend and I will also not call you. Happy". Charlie calmed down and said, "I will see you on Wednesday morning". Charlie turned away and didn't look at Krishna. Krishna had no choice but to oblige and grinded his teeth in silent fury as Charlie walked away. Krishna walked into kitchen and explained the chef about the special order as he was looking at Charlie thru the corner of his eye. Charlie continued working without looking at Krishna. Krishna's phone rang and he answered, it was a hoarse voice, "hello, is this Krishna?" Krishna was advising the chef and at the same time watching Charlie, so he didn't focus on the voice. The only thing he heard was, "can you come now?" and he immediately obliged and said, "ok, just send me the location". He disconnected the phone, informed the chef about the time that the dish should get ready and told him that it was a really special order, looked at Charlie and shouted, "Charlie, I am leaving now. If there is anything call me". Charlie didn't respond and Krishna left.

Krishna didn't want to leave and actually wanted to be with the chef while preparing the chicken biriyani but since Charlie irritated him, he just wanted to leave the restaurant. The location was near his restaurant and so he reached within ten minutes. When he knocked the door, a young boy aged around 18 opened the door. Krishna became conscious and asked questioningly, "Sorry, is this

Radhika's house?" The boy looked tired and was drowsy and replied with a forced smile, "yes, it is sir. Please come in and sit". The house was well maintained and had marble flooring. The cushions were of a rich fabric and there was a large sized television. Krishna hesitantly entered this plush house and sat down. The boy sat in front of him and started crying. Krishna didn't understand what was happening and the boy spoke, "sir, I was the one who called. I am sorry. I am a homosexual and am having a difficult time with myself. I am not able to tell my parents or anyone for that matter about my condition. I just needed someone to confide in and have been sexually frustrated. If you had not come, then I would have committed suicide".

The last word rung hard in Krishna's ears. His eyes went wide open. His gut feeling made him peep into the bedroom and found a rope hanging off the fan. He rushed towards the boy and slapped him hard and looked furiously at him. The boy almost felt off the sofa. He held the boy's T-shirt with both his hands, lifted him off the sofa and pushed him against the wall and chocked him with all his might. The boy continued crying but now in pain. Krishna continued chocking him and was furious at him, the boy struggled hard to get himself free and said in broken words as he struggled to breathe, "sir,, what are,, what,, doing?" Krishna continued for a few seconds and dropped him. The boy gasped for breath and coughed vigorously. Krishna also took deep breaths and slapped the boy again and shouted, "if suicide is the solution for every problem then everyone in this world should commit suicide". Krishna continued angrily, "is this what you want?", and kissed the boy on his lips for a few seconds.

Krishna went inside the kitchen, had some water, removed the rope from the bedroom and sat on the sofa. As the boy struggled towards the sofa and sat, the door bell rang. Before the boy could realize, Krishna opened the door and boy's parents were a little surprised to see a stranger open the door. The boy quickly wiped his face with his T-shirt and got up. "Who are you?", asked Krishna nonchalantly. The boy's father surprisingly replied, "we are supposed to ask you that question. Where's Krishna and who are you?" Krishna had a small smile on his face and turned towards the boy. The boy Krishna walked hesitatingly towards the door as he said, "Ma, this is my friend...", Krishna waved his hand, interrupted the boy and looked at the parents and told in a stern tone, "Look, sir and madam, I am your son's friend. Your son has been suffering for years and you have failed to realize. You would have lost him by now. He tried to commit to suicide", Krishna pointed his finger towards the rope.

The boy's face was white with fear as the parents broke down and rushed towards the boy. All three started crying loudly as Krishna shut the door. Krishna sat on the sofa and took deep breaths. He was observing the three of them as the parents went thru different emotions; the mother slapped the boy and hugged him. The father took the boy with his collar and asked the same 'why' in different tones. The boy didn't reply as the father walked towards Krishna with folding hands. Krishna said, "Sir, your son is a homosexual". The father was puzzled and asked what it meant. Krishna took a deep breath, made the boy's parents sit on the sofa and the boy opposite to them. Krishna explained calmly, "See, basically just like a child is born with physical deformities, a child can be born with mental deformities. Actually it is not a deformity, we feel that we are normal and they are not, its just that they are different. Anyways, back to the point and to put it in a simple language for you to comprehend, your son's wiring inside the brain is different. So he likes men instead of women". On hearing this, more tears rolled out from all the three. The mother stopped looking at Krishna and put her face in her hands. The father continued listening calmly. "There's nothing wrong with it, its just different. I think technically a doctor will be able to help you understand better. Don't worry, its natural. Animals exhibit this as well, elephants, zebras and many others". The father tried controlling his tears and asked puzzlingly, "is there any medicine which will cure this?"

Krishna smiled and said, "is there any medicine that can grow back a person's hand if he was not born with it? Well again, let me tell you three things: I am not a doctor so please talk to one very soon to understand his situation technically. Second, this is completely natural and there's nothing to worry about it. Its unfortunate that many of us are not aware and live either in a state of despair or end up taking a bold step like your son. Third, please don't resort to black magic or witchcraft after consulting a doctor". Krishna got a message from Satya, "is the plan still on?" He got up and replied to the message. The parents and the boy got up. The parents folded their hands again. Krishna hugged the boy and left. As he walked away, the father told, "we will consult a doctor soon and will see what needs to be done next. Thank you for saving our son. By the way, whats your name?". "Well, thank you for understanding the state of your son, Krishna", smiled Krishna as he stressed on the last word and walked away.

Krishna reached the restaurant, tasted the dish, packed more food and left for his home. He didn't find Charlie around but was not bothered. After getting ready he informed Satya that he was leaving and got a call, it was Radha. He hesitantly picked it up, "Hi Krishna, how come you are so busy. Its been a while since we met. Why don't we meet today?" He was irritated and replied with a smile, "well actually I am going to my friends place and am busy with finalizing the details of the new restaurant. So lets try to meet later". "Ok fine, then Saturday night. I found this new pub which opened, will send you the details, please join", came the reply. Krishna acknowledged and left. As he was on the way to Satya's house, he was wondering, "does Radha like me or is she trying to use me so that she could spend her time. Why is she behind me to meet every other week? Why am I trying to avoid her? I just helped her the other day when in need. I have been helping others as well. It is becoming difficult to understand this woman. Do I like Radha subconsciously and not able to understand? I am confused".

Satya wore a red skirt with a white top and was radiating. As Krishna entered the house, he said, "oh, looking gorgeous. And you have bought some lights for tonight. So who else is coming, any of your office colleagues. There's enough food that I got". Saytabama blushed and said, "thanks and this evening is actually special for me than for you. This is an evening for you Krishna and only you". Krishna smiled and sat down. Satya got the vodka bottle and the glasses. Krishna made the drink and as he clinked the glass, Satya said, "to cancer", and before Krishna could say anything she gulped the entire glass. Krishna said, "Look, this is going to be a long evening. So please don't spoil it by getting a headache. Take it slow". She didn't reply anything and lit a cigarette and looked outside. She continued smoking and had tears as Krishna slowly had his drink. After finishing the cigarette, she took a deep sigh, wiped her tears, smiled and said, "ok, sorry. I will be fine". So tell me, how was your day. How is your new restaurant coming up?". Krishna looked into her eyes and said, "I really need to learn this trick from you girls. You can cry at the snap of a finger and stop at a snap of a finger". Satya started laughing and said, "well, then you tell me. How many girls have you seen who cry at the snap of a finger?".

Krishna told about Abhinaya and few other customers that he met and ended with Radha. After completing three rounds of drinks and a packet of cigarettes, Satya looked at Krishna and said, "Radha likes you Krishna. She will propose to you soon". Krishna's was shocked to hear this and said, "hey, hold on, hold on. This is the first time I am telling you about her. And also, I am meeting you for the second time. How in this world can you come to this conclusion?" Satya winked to him and said, "I will be the first person you will call and tell when she proposes to you". It became around 1 in the night and both continued chatting; Satya about her school, college, work & friends, and Krishna about his restaurant, Abhinaya and his other sisters. Only one-fourth of the bottle was left when Krishna asked, "do you want to try ganja?" Satya's eyes grew wide open with excitement, "why didn't you tell me before?" After completing the joint, she came close to him and whispered, "is there anything else that you would like to show me?" and kissed him. Both kissed passionately for a long time on the floor, removed their clothes and continued kissing. They went into the bathroom and ended up making love under the shower.

Krishna got up the next morning and heard two sounds, Satya making something in the kitchen and his phone vibrating. He answered the call without seeing who it was and heard, "Krishna where the hell are you? Do you know what time is it?" Krishna was wondering who was shouting at him and was shocked to see the time was 1030. It was Charlie's voice, "Krishna I told you yesterday that the electrician guys would come at 1030 at the new place. What the hell are you doing? You told me that you wouldn't call me but that doesn't mean that I would stop calling you". Krishna took a moment to realize what Charlie was telling and he continued, "Look I had a long call with Abhinaya and you handle it now" and disconnected the call. Krishna fumed with anger as Satya entered. Krishna forced a smile at her and continued talking on the phone with a bossy tone, "Look Charlie, I will handle it. Don't worry about it. It's a piece of cake".

She burst into laughter and said, "Why do you fake it Krishna, the line got disconnected when I came?" Krishna felt embarrassed and covered his face. She came close to him and pushed his hands away said with a smile, "When the call gets disconnected, the backlight glows. Now have your coffee". She sat in front of him, sipped her coffee and observed him as he made some frantic calls, got the situation under control and was surprised to see

Abhinaya's missed call. He called her back and told her that he had the situation under control, and would give all the details the next time she was here. Krishna had his coffee and told, "I really need to leave. Its late and there's lot of work". Satya said, "Look Krishna, thanks for everything. I am going thru a roller coaster of emotions and to add on, my days are numbered". He came close to her and put his finger on her mouth and said, "Don't tell me that line again. Life is like a box of chocolates, you never know what you gonna get. Forrest Gump said that. So believe in that. Magic happens. And I would like to tell you something. I am actually very careful and have been ever since I started. But yesterday was the first time I didn't put on a condom. It just slipped my mind". She winked at him, "Now please don't tell me that I will also have AIDS along with cancer". Krishna smiled and replied, "I get myself tested every second week. I am fine and so will you be. But I thought I should let you know about this". Satya hugged him and said, "So, will I get pregnant now"?

Krishna pushed her as he smiled, but Satya again hugged him and said, "I will definitely reduce my smoking Krishna but this stress is killing me". She continued hugging him and had tears. He replied, "Teach me how to cry at the snap of a finger and I will teach you how to tackle stress". She pushed him away and said, "How did you know I was crying?" He winked at her and asked, "How do you know that Radha will propose to me?" She smiled and said, "Krishna, please take care of yourself. I really don't know why you started being a gigolo but you should stop now. I am sure you would have had fun in the beginning but after sometime it is a big monotony. Going by what you said and from whatever I know you, Radha definitely likes you and you should also give it a try. If you are confused take your time but she's clear from her side. You supported her when she needed you the most and that clicked for her. That's what every girl wants, healthy understanding. You are a good listener Krishna, you listen with your soul and mind, not with your heart and brain". Krishna had a twinkle in the eye when he heard the last sentence. He replied, "ok, fine. Three things for you: no negativity, no smoking and call me if anything is needed".

Krishna reached the new location and attended the electrician. Later he went to the restaurant and continued with the work there. He became so busy that he couldn't reply to Radha's call. Later in the evening he messaged her that he would not be able to make it. She called him five times and even Abhinaya called him three times. At that moment he felt Charlie was a great asset and there was no point in instigating him unnecessarily. At the end of the day he was so tired that he slept off without changing. The next few days kept him busy and on Wednesday when Charlie came, he didn't smile at Krishna. Krishna was irritated but kept his cool, walked up to him and asked "Charlie, how are your kids? Hope you had a good break". "All is well Krishna, how about you, how was work, pretty busy I guess", replied Charlie heedlessly. Krishna forced a smile and said, "well Charlie, who knows that better than you. Now that you are back, I have some breathing space". Charlie smiled at him and both continued their discussion on work. Krishna briefed him the details and left home. He had a long sleep in the afternoon and that was a much needed rest after a tiring week. Just as he was about to get up in the evening, he got a call. In the state of drowsiness, he didn't realize who it was as the voice sounded child-like, "Is this Krishna?" Krishna just hummed without answering. Without hearing properly, he replied, "send me the location details and time". The request was for the early evening and the address was nearby. He messaged Charlie that he would be late, packed his bag, got ready and left.

It was around 7 and when he knocked the door, he heard the same child-like voice, "who is it?" Krishna became a little conscious as he slowly opened the door, "Well, this is Krishna, you called me around an hour ago". The reply was, "Thanks for coming but you can leave. Close the door hard and leave", the sentence ended in a rude tone. Krishna now got used to these types of replies. His eyes were searching hard to identify this lady but couldn't find her. She asked angrily, "what are you waiting for? You don't want to leave. Shall I call the police?" Krishna replied calmly, "look madam, you are one who called me and despite this you want to call the police then I have no problem, please go ahead. But hear me out for a minute. I honestly don't know why I became a gigolo but I have done my job exceedingly well to the best of my efforts. I have satisfied women of all age groups upto 65. I have satisfied a male homosexual and I have even consulted a transgender. So if you still think you don't need me I will leave." He didn't receive any response for a few seconds and as he was just about to leave a dwarf lady, barely 4 feet, ran towards him crying. This was the biggest shocker to Krishna since he started this 'other activity' but controlled his emotions at his best. As she came running towards him, he knelt down and opened his arms. She hugged him and cried inconsolably. Krishna said softly, "when you are not keeping well, you go to a doctor and you get the same medication as any other human being gets. So the doctor treats your disease and doesn't cares about the physical appearance. Likewise I have to follow my Hippocratic oath, that is, to provide my service to meet your needs. So tell me, what is your name?" "Sandhya", she kept repeating her name many times. As he tried to push her away she continued crying and continued hugging him. Krishna said, "All that a human being needs is self-respect and looks like you are devoid of that at many places". Sandhya slowly stopped crying and kissed Krishna. She kissed him passionately, Krishna sucked her tongue and it sent her into a tizzy; and both ended up having sex.

"Well luckily I read about the challenges that little people face in their sexual needs and the different sexual positions to actually help little people, so looks like reading helps", quipped Krishna. Sandhya hugged him and said," Krishna, you first respected me as a fellow human being. Second, you respected my feelings. Third, you satisfied my needs more than I could imagine. I cannot ask for anything more. You are definitely unique Krishna". Krishna smiled and replied, "well thanks and I will leave now. I have told my staff that I will reach by 8". Sandhya took the money from her bag and said, "here's your payment". Krishna took the vibrator from his bag and gave it to her and said in a serious tone, "I will be honest with you. A so called 'normal' person will not come and sleep with you. So, you use this. It will be your best friend. This is actually my second one. I gave the first one to a transgender, Aravind. I met her similarly when she called me to her house. The moment I gave this self-respect speech, she broke into tears and hugged me and kissed me. She said she didn't want anything else but someone to talk to intimately, that's all. So I gave her the vibrator and told her that it was her best friend and didn't take any money. So please don't feel bad, I will not take the money. If I feel I have genuinely made an impact then I don't like taking money". Sandhya had tears, didn't want to argue with him, took the vibrator and kissed him on his forehead and said, "Krishna, you are very nice human being, whoever marries you is very gifted to have you".

As Krishna started his bike to leave to the restaurant, he saw a message from Radha asking him if they could meet him. He had tears in his eyes as he started his bike and drove towards the restaurant. He had a mix of thoughts while driving, "what am I doing with my life? Why did I start all this? I don't know whether what I am doing is right or wrong? But I am actually making people feel happy. By giving happiness we get happiness, isn't it? I have many people who are telling that Radha is the right person for me whereas I am not still not sure. Maybe if I spend more time with her I will be more sure. She's been trying to meet me and I am avoiding her. I have time for my 'other activity' but no time for her. Is this right or wrong? Should I settle down now with Radha as I am the last to get married amongst all my cousins? I don't know whether I am good enough for her. Will she accept me, especially with the fact that I have been continuing my 'other activity' since the last five months after knowing her. But how long do I continue this. It has become monotonous and also there is a huge health risk. Also sometimes I don't get to ejaculate and it pains. And sometimes I ejaculate early but the women would want me to continue. Maybe I should give this a break and decide whether to continue or not. I am confused". Krishna's tears continued till he reached the restaurant. As he was parking his bike, Charlie observed him and asked, "Krishna is everything alright?" Krishna didn't look at him and replied, "Lets get to work Charlie, we have a long night".

After a couple of days Krishna met Vivek and his father to brief the details of the new cloud kitchen and a small inauguration event that they had planned. All were satisfied and the first thing Krishna did is call Radha and hesitantly said, "Hi Radha". "Sorry, wrong number", came a quick reply and the line got disconnected. Krishna was surprised and rechecked if he dialed the correct number and called again. Before he could say something, "oh my god Krishna, is it really you? I thought you dialed my number by mistake. Is everything all right as you are calling me after a long time?". Krishna took a long pause and said, "sorry Radha. My sincere apologies. I was busy with work and couldn't join you for any of your outings or pubs. And also I was not in touch with you. Actually I have been in less touch with Abhinaya as well. So please accept my apologies" Radha replied, "oh my god, did you actually write down whatever you said and prepared before talking to me", and started laughing further. "Ok, apologies accepted and yes I cut your call on purpose. Just kidding. So tell me how are you? What is keeping you busy? How is the new cloud kitchen coming up?" Krishna replied, "listen are you free tomorrow afternoon? If so, please come for the inauguration of the cloud kitchen. I will send you the details".

It was 1230 in the afternoon and the cloud kitchen was ready for its opening. Radha was decked up in a green silk saree and Krishna just couldn't take eyes off her. Radha noticed Krishna, winked at him and asked, "How's the babe looking?" Krishna looked past her, to the sides, behind, and replied casually, "I don't see any babe around". Radha giggled, patted his cheek and asked again, "How's the babe looking?". Krishna looked straight into her eyes and lip-synced, "awesome". Vivek noticed all of this and walked towards them, Krishna introduced both of them and Vivek pulled Krishna aside. Radha was talking to the chef and the staff. "Krishna, who's this? Where's Abhinaya? I thought we decided she would light the first kitchen fire", asked Vivek in an irritating tone. As Krishna was about to reply, Charlie barged into their conversation, smiled and said, "Krishna, do you want me to tell about the other phone calls that you keep getting?"

Krishna fumed with anger, controlled himself and as Charlie left, replied calmly to Vivek, "Look, Abhinaya is in Brussels on a consulting project. It was sudden and since she was already in Paris, the company asked her to move there immediately. Else she would have come. Yes, she was supposed to light the first fire but its ok. Let Radha do this. Even she does not knows about it. Trust me on what I am doing. By the way, for the records, she is still just a friend, ok", Krishna looked sternly into Vivek's eyes. Radha interrupted their conversation, "Krishna, so what's cooking for lunch? By the way Vivek, Krishna did mention about you to me. I am amazed at how you are able to handle so many businesses". Vivek replied with a smile, "well, I guess its in the genes. But yes, Krishna does all the work really well so I can focus on other businesses. But Krishna, what was Charlie telling about the phone calls, are you trying to start something else on your own? If so, please do make me as a partner, big guy". Vivek mocked at Krishna in the end and Krishna blushed, before he could reply anything Radha puzzling asked, "So Krishna, whats this phone calls about? Is this some call centre you have setup? Is this the reason why you are trying to avoid my calls?" Krishna tried to reply and again got interrupted by Charlie as he shouted, "Hello everyone, please come over. We have a special guest tonight and the first kitchen fire will be lit by Radha". Radha was pleasantly surprised by this gesture and looked at Krishna, he reacted in a manner which could be easily interpreted as, "hey, don't look at me like that".

After the ceremonial boiling of milk, lunch that was ordered from outside was served to all staff who came from the other restaurant, the new staff at the cloud kitchen and in the end Vivek, Krishna and Radha sat down for lunch. Krishna explained about Vivek's businesses, how they ended up starting the restaurant in Adyar and how they came up with this concept of cloud kitchen which was picking up fast owing to the mobile apps that aggregate all the restaurants and provide a wider choice. Radha shared her experiences in Chennai, how she liked the city and hated the city at the same time, and how she met Krishna. As they completed lunch, Vivek bade a goodbye to everyone and wished Radha for her stint in Chennai as he had to leave for other meetings. As he left, he pulled Krishna to the side and asked in a serious tone, "Dude, I am almost sure she likes you. If you share the same feeling then please don't miss this chance. You should be gifted to have someone like her. You know that I liked someone and it didn't work out right. So please think over seriously". Krishna did not know how to react and replied in a confused tone, "what are you.. how do you.. do you even.. how the hell.". and looked at Radha. Vivek held Krishna's hand hard so that it was painful and told angrily, "Krishna, either stop over reacting or don't make a fool out of yourself. Tell me honestly, don't you have any feelings for her?" Krishna slowly pushed away Vivek's hand and said in a slow tone, "I am confused Vivek". Radha barged into their conversation, "Hey Vivek, did you try the ice cream? I know Krishna doesn't likes strawberry flavor. Its very nice. Where did you get it from Krishna?" Krishna gave the cup to Vivek, looked away from both of them and replied, "it's from a new store around the corner" and walked away.

Vivek left after having a chat with Radha. Krishna guided the new staff and took feedback from the old staff on the arrangements at the kitchen. They discussed for around fifteen minutes as Radha was looking at their conversations. Krishna became conscious that he was making Radha wait. Before he could even continue, Charlie interrupted him, smiled and said, "Krishna, why don't you drop her home? I remember you telling me that you had to drop her. I will handle" Krishna smiled and walked towards Radha. "So how long are you planning to make me wait today like how you made me wait all these days without meeting?" winked Radha. Krishna smiled and said, "well, I have made you wait enough and I genuinely apologize. So I am all yours till the night". Radha put her hands over her mouth and said, "oh my god, really. Krishna, is this really you". Krishna immediately replied as he took her hands away from her mouth and said, "look don't overact. I apologize again. Tell me how should I compensate". Radha smiled and said, "ok, apologizes accepted. You know where all I have been. So since you said you are mine the whole of today, you make the plan and I am ok with wherever you take me". Krishna thought for a moment and said, "ok, movie, coffee and pub. So if you have not seen Frozen 2 then lets go for it because I don't want you to repeat the same movie again". Radha replied questioningly, "The plan is excellent but pub in a saree is a little too much". Krishna winked and said, "well, then today is the day you become a modern day Radha. Who said a woman in saree is not allowed in a pub? Isn't it the other way round for pub rules, no round neck tees for men, no open-toe footwear for men, have you ever seen a rule for a woman in a pub?" Radha pushed him away, smiled and said, "oh my god, you are crazy. Lets go".

Radha slept thru most of the movie. Krishna didn't try to wake her up and at the end of the movie he asked her, "so how did you like the movie?" Radha replied apologetically, "Look, I am sorry, I had a long night yesterday at work and was tired. If not for your event today I wouldn't have left the house. I was planning to sleep the whole of afternoon". Krishna smiled and replied, "looks like the sambhar rice added to your sleep". She giggled and said, "ok fine, so can we go to the beach and then to the pub. I want to enjoy some fresh breeze". As they drove to the beach, Radha explained her work to Krishna and he questioned her occasionally. The same continued while spending time in the beach as well. As they were driving back to a new pub which Krishna discovered, Radha asked, "Hey Krishna, tell me one thing. What do think of me?" Krishna was shocked to hear this. He looked at her but didn't loose focus on the road. He smiled and replied, "Sorry, whats wrong with you? What kind of a question is that?" She looked straight at him as said, "No, I mean just like that, I wanted to understand what you feel about me? I have been trying to reach you many times over a call and tried to meet you many times. You helped me when I was really down in my life and it was a really great thing that happened to me at that time. So I genuinely felt that I should do something for you. I don't cook well nor I don't know how I could help you with your work. So that's the reason I kept chasing you to meet you so that at least I feel revealed off the burden in my head and genuinely thank you".

Krishna stopped the car on the side, smiled and said, "Look Radha, at that particular moment I had time. You know what happened right, I was with you but was continuously on the phone and doing my work. Yes, you are right, many wouldn't do that; I agree. I also appreciate the fact that you want to repay me but that's fine. Don't feel overburdened. Let me be honest with you, in the beginning I felt a little irritated but later I figured out that you were feeling obliged. So many a times I was loaded with work and yes there were occasions when I genuinely tried to avoid meeting you. So, I am apologizing again for the same. But now that I have clarified, I am sure you will feel much lighter in your head". Krishna took a pause and was contemplating whether to tell about his 'other activity'. Was is it the right time? He was not sure. Radha heaved a sigh of relief and before she could say anything he replied, "yes, there's one more thing that I wanted to tell…" He thought it was right time to tell Radha but a car started honking from behind indicating that they needed to park on the side where Radha's car was. So Krishna immediately moved the car a little forward and stopped. Radha pinched his cheek and said with a wide smile, "Thanks a lot for your honest explanation, I feel really light in my head. So tell me whats the other thing you wanted to tell?" Krishna paused for a moment and decided this was not the time and replied, "Today you pay the bill", and started laughing. She hit him on his shoulder and asked him to drive.

All eyes in the pub were on Radha as she was the only one wearing a saree. She felt conscious and told Krishna irritatingly, "At least we could have gone home and changed. This is so mean. Everyone is looking at me". As she completed the sentence, she took a bottoms up of her drink. Krishna knew she was angry with him and went close to her and said, "If you had come to my house then you would have had no choice but my clothes. If we went to your place then you would have taken an hour for changing and make up. So I decided this is the best", and started laughing. She hit him again on the shoulder and smiled and said, "you really know how to handle any situation. Ok, go ahead and order whatever you want since I am paying. Let me guess, pineapple juice for you since you are driving. By the way, how's Abhinaya doing, its been a while since I spoke to her or even chatted with her". "She's fine. She's in Brussels. I suggested to her to spend the New year there itself. It is better there with all the Christmas lighting and decorations. Just that she needs to be alert on this new virus that could spread globally", replied Krishna as he indicated to the waiter. He ordered food, drinks and told about Abdul, how they met and decided to live together for sometime before getting married. "I know about Abhinaya, she wont care a damn. But I am surprised, how come his parents have no objection, I mean different religion and to top it all, live-in", asked Radha puzzlingly as she completed her third drink. "Well, he has his own share of problems. Both his sisters are divorced as they had terrible husbands. So his parents told him to do whatever he wants, they are happy as long as he gets married", smiled Krishna.

"Lucky him, actually lucky both", replied Radha as she got up and pulled him to the dance floor. She forced him to dance but Krishna was not comfortable. Both enjoyed the music for sometime and it became 11. Radha had five rounds of vodka and Krishna helped her to the car. As Krishna drove her to her house she was fiddling with the radio and grooving to a few songs. Krishna didn't bother much and when they reached Radha looked at Krishna and asked in a serious tone, "Krishna, will you marry me?" Krishna was shocked to hear this and was looking thru into her eyes to see if she was blabbering but he knew what she was talking. She continued in a serious tone, "Krishna, I had five rounds of vodka but I know what I am talking. Will you marry me?"

Krishna was still puzzled as tears started rolling down his eyes. Radha smiled and came towards him and kissed him. It was barely for five seconds when Krishna's phone rang and as he tried reaching his phone Radha kissed him harder and moved towards him. Krishna cut the call but the phone rang again. This time Radha moved back and was surprised to see Krishna tears, smiled and said, "oh my god, today seems to be a role reversal. I proposed, I initiated the kiss and you are crying". Krishna replied, "yes, I am blessed to have someone wanting me so much. At the end of the day, that's what people want". Krishna's phone rang again, and he cut the call. "Looks like someone is not liking this moment", smiled Krishna as he wiped his tears. "Well, why don't you come home and have a drink, may be after that you can stay over because you don't drink and drive", asked Radha in sly tone and winked. Krishna replied, "So looks like the role reversal still continues with you wanting wild sex". Radha blushed, hit him on his shoulder and pushed him away and said, "ok fine go away. Anyway, you are continuously getting calls". Krishna's phone rang again, he got irritated and got out of the car and walked away to pick up the call and asked in an angry tone, "who's this"?

A childish voice replied, "hi, this is Deepa. Remember you came to my house once". Krishna tried hard to recollect amongst the many customers who could this be. Yes, there was a Deepa, but her tone was very sweet as compared to this childish voice. "Listen, sorry to call you many times but I need a help from you". Krishna cut her short and said, "Sorry, I stopped whatever you are asking for". While telling this he looked at Radha, she was waiting for him eagerly at the gate. He realized that his reply was so spontaneous, and at that very moment, confirming to himself the fact that he was committed. It came to him so naturally. He realized that moment that she's the one and Vivek was right; so were the others but the major question lingering in his head was how to reveal his 'other activity' to her. "Sir, are you still there? Sorry, this is nothing to do with pleasure. This is a life and death situation. I barely know anyone in this city. And at this time of the night I am stuck. My friend is badly injured and needs medical attention. Please help". Krishna hesitantly replied, "look Deepa I understand but I am in the middle of something important and it is very difficult to come. If you want I can arrange for a doctor to visit or get an ambulance. Let me start coordinating.".. The childish voice cut him short, "sir, please. I can call an ambulance myself but I need some support now. This is in OMR, my friends place. Please help". Krishna took a pause, realized that he was nearby and replied, "ok send me the address. I will come".

Krishna walked towards Radha as she got down from the car and said, "hey look. Sorry I need to leave. Some medical emergency for a friend". Radha got concerned, "hey, is anything serious? Do you want to take my car?" Krishna replied slowly, "Car – no. Serious – I don't think so. Sorry – yes, really sorry that I have to leave like this". Radha smiled and asked, "you are still yet to reply to my question?" Krishna trying to avoid answering the question, replied slowly, "Look Radha, like I said I am gifted to have someone liking me so much but I need to tell you something". Radha immediately replied, "Oh my god Krishna, come on, this is very filmy. This dialogue comes in many movies. Try something else", and started laughing. As Krishna opened his mouth, his phone rang again and heard, "sir, I sent you the address, did you check, can you please come fast? She's bleeding". Radha said, "ok go for now. But I am waiting for the answer". Krishna smiled and said, "And I am waiting for the wild ssss…" Radha giggled, pushed him away and kept her index finger on her lips and started walking away. She turned back, bade him a goodbye, a flying kiss and went to her house. Krishna took an auto that was passing by and the moment he sat, tears started rolling down his eyes.

Chapter 7

DENOUEMENT

Krishna went to the address. It was a small building with four houses. The streetlights were not functioning properly from this house till the end of the road. He checked the house number again on the address and found that it was the house on the ground floor. When he rang the bell, there was no answer. He knocked the door and again there was no answer. He knocked again, and as he knocked a fat man at his back held his right hand tightly and placed a knife on Krishna's back. Krishna was shocked and his face turned white with fear. The fat man whispered in Krishna's ears, "if you scream, I will force this knife between your buttocks. Just walk into the house". Another fat man opened the door from the inside of the house and first person pushed Krishna to the floor. Before he could tell anything, the second person tied Krishna hands by placing them behind him and the first person started tying Krishna's mouth with a cloth. Krishna figured out what was happening, started crying and pleaded them to leave him, he promised he would run away and not inform anyone, he fell on their feet and as the two started overpowering Krishna, he mouthed foul words and started threatening them. Before Krishna could tell anything the second person finished tying his mouth with a cloth. Everything happened within a few seconds. They were ready to sodomize him.

Both the men removed their pants and pulled Krishna's pants. The first fat man started forcing his penis in Krishna's anus while the second fat man started patting his penis on Krishna's face. Krishna tried to make the loudest sounds possible, move as vigorously as possible and tried moving away from them but when that happened the second person started beating Krishna with a wooden stick on his lower back and buttocks. Krishna screamed in pain and became helpless. The second fat man came close to Krishna's face and said, "if you cooperate we can finish in five minutes, else we will ensure that you will bleed to death here". Krishna cried badly and stopped moving and the first fat man inserted his penis so hard that he felt dizzy for a moment. "Oh my god, its so tight and nice," told the first fat man to the second fat man as he moved his penis inside out vigorously while the second fat man continued patting his penis on Krishna's face. After a couple of minutes the first fat man ejaculated and both switched places. After another couple of minutes the second fat man ejaculated and told to the first, "its been months since we did this right. And this dude cooperated well". After their wore their pants the first fat man removed the knot from Krishna's hands and told him, "look, we said five minutes and done. You cooperated well. Now you better leave from here in another five minutes. The people in this house have gone for a movie and will come back now anytime". Krishna continued crying, his muffled sounds changed from help to pain to helplessness.

Krishna couldn't stand as it was extremely painful. He continued crying in pain as he wore his pants lying on floor. He touched his derriere and found lot of blood. The first thing he did was to leave that house and move to another street. He struggled to walk and kept falling down. He was conscious to observe everywhere so that no was seeing him. He tried his best to walk normally but it was extremely painful. As he reached another street where there was light, he sat on the footpath as he couldn't stand and called Regina. He spoke slowly so that he could control his tears, "Hello madam. This is Krishna. Hope you remember me". Regina had a wide smile as she replied, "Oh Krishna, of course I remember you. How can I forget you? What happened, why are you calling up so late? You woke me up from my sleep Krishna. Everything alright". Krishna couldn't control his tears, "Sorry madam. I am hurt and I didn't know anyone to call. I need your help". Regina was very worried, "Oh Krishna, what happened, are you ok? Is it serious? Why are you crying?" Krishna continued in tears, "I will tell you when I meet you madam, sorry cant tell over phone. I am bleeding and need hospitalization. But otherwise I am fine, I can walk". Regina got more worried, "ok Krishna, come to the railway hospital immediately. Put pressure on the wound so that bleeding stops. I will reach the hospital in twenty minutes".

As Regina kept the phone, there was a message from Radha, "Hi, what happened, everything alright? I am waiting for your call". Krishna burst into tears and dropped the phone on the road. Immediately he picked up the phone and replied to her, "sorry, cant call. It was an emergency. Need to move him to another hospital. Will call you tomorrow. Please sleep". He then booked a cab which came within a minute. He lied down in the backseat and started crying loudly. The driver stopped the car and Krishna shouted, "please go to the railway hospital fast. I am alright. I am crying for my own actions".

Throughout the journey Krishna kept crying and the driver drove as fast as he could. All negative thoughts ran through Krishna's mind; his decision to come back from the USA when everyone told him to try for jobs there, fights with his father and moving out of the house, the way he never used to listen to Abhinaya, and the way he ignored Radha. As they reached the hospital, Regina was waiting there. Krishna struggled to get out of the car and as Regina held him she could feel the pant wet. The car seat had blood stains. The driver got concerned, immediately Krishna gave 2000 rupees to the driver and said, "sorry sir, please use this money for cleaning". The driver denied, but Krishna dropped the money inside the car and closed the door. Regina understood what happened and had tears; on seeing her Krishna replied, "I have to pay for my actions Regina madam. You know what has happened and how can I take my family's help for this?" Regina didn't reply and wiped her tears. They went to the emergency ward and Regina got Krishna sedated.

Krishna got up in the afternoon the next day and was feeling drowsy. Regina was praying next to him and didn't see him get up. Krishna waited for a moment and when Regina saw him, tears started rolling down her cheeks. She cried continuously and Krishna didn't understand what happened. He saw the wall and figured out that its been more than twelve hours since he had been in the hospital. Krishna kept his hands on Regina's and said, "Look ma'am, you told me I had a gift of making people happy. So I made two men happy yesterday and this is result". Regina smiled for the first time and tears stopped. But she continued to look worried. A doctor entered with a wide smile and said, "Hello Krishna, how are you? How are you feeling now? I am Dr.Rajkiran. Please lie down". Gathering some strength, Krishna said, "hello doctor, I am feeling numb down there, otherwise I am feeling hungry". Dr.Rajkiran replied, "Oh that's good, yes hunger is very good". He looked at Regina and asked, "so, did you…?" Regina nodded her head, burst into tears and went outside the room. Krishna was surprised and asked, "what happened?" Dr.Rajkiran laughed and said, "well you know how woman are, they can cry at the drop of a hat". Krishna laughed and said, "well, exactly. I told Regina ma'am the same thing when I met her".

Dr.Rajkiran continued, "So Krishna, here's the deal. I know what happened; well actually I figured out what happened. You have some stiches down there in your anus, that's the reason for the numbness. And you will feel pain whenever you pass your stools for the next one week. So please take the medicines and apply cream down there, you can stop once the pain subsides". Krishna laughed and replied, "Oh my god, that's it. Regina cried so much for this?" Dr.Rajkiran pulled a chair and sat next to him and said, "well Krishna she didn't cry for that. Ok, she cried for that and something more as well. Your injury is a minor issue and will get set in a week's time, maybe ten days. But when we went thru the ultrasound yesterday just to ensure that you didn't have any internal injury we found a tumor. So today morning we did a CT scan to double check what this tumor is and how big is it". Dr.Rajkiran took a pause, came closer to Krishna and said, "look Krishna, everyone has tumors in our body. Most of them are benign and don't need any treatment and some are treatable. But some tumors grow. Yours is that type". Krishna had no clue what was being told to him. He was listening patiently. Dr.Rajkiran knew that Krishna was not understanding what he was telling, he held Krishna's hand, looked into his eyes and said, "you have stomach cancer Krishna, its stage 3".

Krishna was speechless and completely shattered, held Dr.Rajkiran's hand very tightly with both his hands and had tears rolling down his cheeks. He couldn't believe what the doctor said, and words were not coming out of his mouth, "Doctor, I … I … are you…. are you… sure?" The doctor's hand was paining but he didn't react, he was patiently waiting for Krishna to complete. He said emotionlessly, "yes, Krishna, I am 99% sure. The other 1% I leave to the biopsy report for confirmation and to understand what kind of tumor it is. Thereby we can also figure out which medicine to be given for chemotherapy". Krishna immediately dropped the doctor's hand and cried out loudly. Regina came running in and hugged him, both cried inconsolably. Dr.Rajkiran patiently observed everything. After a couple of minutes, both reconciled themselves.

Dr.Rajkiran continued, "Krishna, listen patiently. I will tell you three things. First, there's no reason for cancer. My father smoked for 40 years and is fine whereas my mother who never smoked died of throat cancer a few years ago. So don't have a feeling that, oh I used to smoke so I got it or I used to binge drink so I got it. All said and done smoking is a no go, absolutely no smoking. Second, the faster you accept it and the faster you get into medication, the better it is. Luckily many of your other parameters are fine, so it means it is treatable. Third is the most important thing, have a positive outlook towards life. Be grateful that you can afford this, which I presume you can based on what Regina told me. Stay positive and tell yourself that you can overcome this and after overcoming this, promise to yourself that you will work more harder to help others. Going thru this journey will only open up your perspective towards philanthropy. Ok enough wisdom for today. Can I leave?... Sorry, any questions?" smiled Dr.Rajkiran as he stopped talking.

Krishna emotionlessly asked, "whats the guarantee that this will be cured doctor?" Dr.Rajkiran laughed and said, "don't take me wrong Krishna. I don't want to be the villain in this room but when you leave in another one hour do you have a guarantee that you will not die in a road accident, or will there not be an earthquake tomorrow in Chennai. So to answer your question, the success rate is around 75%. See, I didn't tell you that the failure rate is 25%. Hope, Krishna. Hope is everything. Lets hope that everything will go good and work towards it with full determination. I heard that you are in the restaurant business and you started a new cloud kitchen. You started hoping that you will succeed right. If you had a doubt of failure you would not have started. So hope keeps driving us. Lets hope that you fall in the 75% window. Ok? Any more questions?" Krishna nodded, looked at Regina and smiled and had tears.

The doctor left, Regina walked with him outside, ordered for food and came back. She asked in a soft tone, "Krishna, when will you tell your parents? Do you want me to come along when you inform them?" Krishna replied, "Madam, I will of course have to tell them but not now. Let me think over it. Now this news has killed my hunger. But Dr.Rajkiran is right, not eating will lead to poor health and fighting the disease will become more difficult and the vicious cycle continues. So please give me some time to think over. And of course thanks a ton for your help. I don't know how to repay you for this", Krishna had tears as he completed. Regina smiled and said, "Krishna, you are copying my dialogue. This is not fair. I told the same thing when we met last time. So please be innovative".

Krishna smiled and started having his food. Regina left the room and indicated to him to ring the bell in case anything is needed. Krishna continued eating while checking his messages. There were four missed calls from Radha, few messages from Vivek, Charlie and Abhinaya. He replied to each of them and called Radha. "Hey Krishna, anything serious. Why are you not answering the phone? After yesterday evening are you planning to continue the same pattern of not answering?", asked Radha in a serious tone. Krishna didn't know what to tell, he had to answer her question on marriage, had to tell her about his 'other activity', had to tell her about the yesterday night's horrific event and also about cancer. He didn't know where to start. "Krishna, can you hear me? You are not answering again", asked Radha in a serious tone. Krishna spoke in a soft tone while looking at himself into the mirror, "hey Radha, relax. I am in the hospital. This friend of mine was injured in his lower back and while treating that they did some tests which revealed he had stomach cancer. Its really shocking but just trying to console him and be with him. You know what, his name is Krishna too", Krishna forced a laugh in the end. Radha replied concerningly, "oh, oh my god. That's crazy. Does he have no one here? This disease is really painful. I have seen my uncle suffering from this". Krishna replied emotionlessly, "Actually its interesting, his girlfriend proposed to him recently and she's far away. Yes, he has no one here. He's thinking how to break this news to his parents". Radha got irritated, "hey come on, he must inform his folks. See I am telling you from my uncle's experience. This disease needs a lot of mental strength. If you have people around then it really matters and is definitely the main need". Krishna paused for a moment and said, "ok I have to go. The doctor has come. I will call you later". Radha replied, "ok take care. But please call me later in the evening".

Krishna got ready and wore the new pants which Regina got. Luckily it fitted him. Both went to the doctor's cabin and met him. Dr.Rajkiran explained the process of chemotherapy and the expenses that he would incur. He suggested a few hospital names in the city where he could consult and told him to call him whenever he had any questions and gave his personal number. Krishna thanked him profusely and left. While in the cab he came to know from Abhinaya that she would be coming in the first week of January to India. He decided to tell her in person. He decided that he will tell his parents also around the same time. He reached home and took a shower. He passed stools for more than twenty minutes as it was painful. He cried silently the whole time. Then he went to the restaurant and spoke with Charlie as if nothing had happened. He was very short in replies as Charlie asked him if everything was alright. Krishna ignored him. Charlie replied, "well what to tell. You always reply like this when you are irritated". Krishna did not get angry at Charlie unlike before where he used to mutter to himself. He smiled as Charlie walked away. Looks like Dr.Rajkiran's positivity is working out, thought Krishna. Then he went to the cloud kitchen to see if things were alright. He stayed there for an hour and called Satya. She was surprised with his call, "hi Krishna, how are you? Long time". Krishna cut her short and said, "I want to meet you, can I come over now?" She replied, "yes sure, is everything ok? Well, sorry, come over. We can talk. I have a bottle ready".

Krishna reached Satya's place and after the pleasantries, he reached for the vodka bottle and asked her if she needed one. He made two strong drinks and before they could even say 'cheers' Krishna gulped the first one down. Satya figured out something was wrong. She didn't say anything, got up and went to the kitchen to get some snacks. By the time she was back with two plates in her hand he finished another drink and was pouring the third one. She came and sat next to him, placed her hands on his shoulder and saw tears rolling down his cheeks, and asked calmly, "what happened to you?" Krishna replied, "I have stomach cancer, stage 3. My first chemotherapy is planned this week". Tears rolled down Satya's cheek. She couldn't believe what she heard. She hugged him tightly and cried loudly. Both cried for a minute and calmed down. She said, "looks like this will be a long night. Sorry, I didn't make any dinner. I was waiting to order food". Krishna cut her short and said, "Your favorite chicken biriyani is there", pointed towards his bag. Both lifted their glasses and clinked them and said in unison, "to cancer" and gulped their drinks. Krishna smiled and said, "last time it was you who said, 'to cancer', and now we told together". Krishna did not mention about sodomy but told about his past stomach pain, medications and how this time the doctors suspected a tumor. Satya heard everything calmly and said, "look Krishna, in my case the chemo medicines are different and yours will be different. So the side effects will be different. But one thing is sure, you will become bald soon", both started laughing.

Both completed the entire bottle of vodka. As they sat down to eat, Krishna told about Radha's proposal. She was so happy for Krishna, got up and hugged him and said, "look I told you the other day itself, you remember right, I told you that she is the one who will propose to you. Look Krishna, its very easy to keep a girl happy. Don't go by the typical forwards on Whatsapp which say women are complicated and difficult to understand". Krishna replied, "ya ya, its easy. But lets see how complicated this gets now. See the moment she told me I stopped taking any sexual requests. It came so naturally to me. I feel that sense of responsibility and commitment. I am usually confused. I haven't told her anything, my medical situation, my 'other activity' and I haven't even responded to her about her proposal". Krishna felt sad as he completed the last sentence and Satya looked at him, kept her hand on his shoulder and said, "Krishna, I haven't told my parents because my case is critical. But like the doctor said your case is different because its treatable. So you have to tell her, tell her everything. Don't hide anything from her Krishna because she's going to be with you forever, you shouldn't have any regrets". Krishna paused for a moment and excused himself to the toilet. He spent more than 25 minutes in pain trying to pass stools and when he came out he saw Satya sleeping. He cleared the plates and slept next to her.

The next morning when Krishna got up Satya was ready with coffee. She asked, "dude, what wrong with you? You vomited or what? I waited for you and slept off". Krishna lied to her saying, "yes, I vomited", as he sipped his coffee. Inside he was feeling the pain in his buttocks and felt guilty. He bade her a goodbye and told her to call him in case of any help. She told him to keep her informed about the doctor's advice. He went all alone to the recommended hospitals, got registered and spoke to the doctors with the reports. He was convinced with the treatment process and the doctors asked if anyone could accompany him. The only person he could think of at that moment was Regina. He still didn't inform his parents. Regina accompanied him for the two days of his first chemotherapy. Post that he stayed in her house for a week which had a round of vomiting sessions, nauseating feeling and tastelessness. He lost almost two kilograms. He coordinated everything over phone with Charlie and as expected Charlie was getting more irritated with Krishna as he had to manage all alone. He received a call from Vivek if everything was alright as Charlie complained to Vivek. Krishna told Vivek not to bother and he was managing everything well. Regina asked him, "Krishna, see I don't have any problem in you staying here for your entire treatment. But please note that you need moral support from your family members. See I don't intend to impinge into your privacy, but parents are important. Ask me, who has experienced the worst". Krishna replied to her calmly, "see madam, I understand whatever you are telling. I will tell them but only after the new year. I need to tell my sister first as she can handle this better than anyone else".

Krishna met Radha in a café, she was excited and said, "oh my god, I am surprised. You called me, you said you wanted to meet and you found a new place. Is this magic?" Krishna smiled and said, "yes, it is magic. So tell me what plans for the new year". "Oh my god Krishna, is it really you? Or is it the aftereffect of my proposal?", Radha stressed slowly on the last word by coming close to him and giggled. Krishna laughed and said, "come on, nothing like that. Actually.". "Hi Krishna, how are you?", interrupted Jayapradha. "Hi Jayapradha, how are you? Oh hey, this is Radha. And Radha, this is Jayapradha, a school teacher. She teaches Tamil". Krishna became conscious. He was nervous how this situation would evolve. Jayapradha also was conscious as to who this girl was and Radha said, "I am his friend….Krishna, come on, you are the one who should introduce me", and giggled. Krishna smiled and said, "sorry, Radha is my friend and…. she is new to the city and wanted to go out to a nice coffee place". The waiter came with two coffees. "Oh yes, Krishna likes coffee a lot. We know each other from the tuitions, that's how I know about this", said Jayapradha. Radha was surprised and eyes grew wide open. Krishna intervened, "Yes, I used to take private tuitions along with Jayapradha", and looked at Jayapradha, "so what's up? Are you with someone?" Jayapradha said, "Yes, that's my fiancé there. I saw you and came to tell you a hello". Krishna looked at him and told Jayapradha, "I am happy for you, all the best". Radha told Jayapradha, "My best wishes". Jayapradha replied immediately, "ok you guys carry on. But one thing Radha, he is a very nice human being", and left.

Radha said, "private tuitions. Krishna you took private tuitions in Tamil". Krishna didn't know what to reply and managed the situation, "no, actually Maths. I like Maths. She's a Tamil teacher. This was in the evening somedays at a place where they teach the underprivileged as a volunteering activity. By the way, what do you want to eat, and yes, what about the new year? Actually I am free and… we could spend time if you want to". Radha kept her hands on her cheeks and said, "oh wow, that's so nice of you. Lets order for burgers. But sorry, this time my new year is with cousins in Bengaluru. All was planned so quickly that I couldn't tell. Since you said we will meet today I thought I will tell you in person". They were interrupted again, "hi Krishna, what a pleasant surprise". Krishna looked up as Kushboo hugged him and then he replied to her, "oh hi Kushboo, how are you? Yes, nice meeting you. By the way this is Radha, a friend of mine who is new to Chennai and wanted to catch up at a nice coffee place. Radha, this is Kushboo, she's the one who did the interiors for the restaurant and the cloud kitchen". Kushboo looked at Radha and waved her hand and was puzzled at what Krishna said, she understood that Krishna was trying to manage the situation and replied, "Yes, that's correct. And ya, I have been very busy lately with good work coming in". She looked at Radha and said, "well, he is a very nice person. I adore him for the respect he has for woman. He helped me with my divorce. Actually I have a potential customer at that table in the corner. Need to go, Krishna I will call you later", and left. Going by the uneasiness that Krishna was feeling, Radha sensed that something was not right but ignored it. Radha came close to Krishna and asked, "you helped her with divorce? So Krishna, I am surprised. Am I meeting a new Krishna or don't I know this side of Krishna? Is this what you wanted to tell me the other day?" Krishna forced a smile and nodded a yes.

Krishna gave very few details possible about Jayapradha and Kushboo, and lied about the Maths tuition and the details of the divorce. He was not feeling comfortable doing this as he was never in such a situation before. They had their burger as Radha told about her cousins and the party that they planned for the new year. She asked, "so Krishna what plans do you have?" Krishna had many things to tell he but couldn't gather the courage to tell her. Just as he was about to reply his phone rang, it was from Satya. "Who's Satya, and why have you stored her number as Satya F no.36. What have you saved my number as?", giggled Radha. Krishna smiled and replied, "I have saved your number as Radha Pune friend. And I am a very organized person, so some people who order food regularly I save in that manner so that it is easy for me to remember". Krishna felt very uneasy as he kept lying to Radha. He wanted to leave the place as early as possible. He said, "ok, so no problem. Please continue with your plan. I am happy for you. Family comes first. That's very nice. I was thinking if you are not doing anything we could spend some time. I have no other specific plans. I was thinking spending time with Abhinaya, but she's back in the 1st week of January. So lets see. Anyway, I have to leave as I have some pending work nearby". Radha was puzzled, "I thought we are spending time now. Please sit for some time because I am leaving tomorrow and will be back by 1st week of January. I need to consume my leaves before they get lapsed". Krishna knew what the next question would be and before Radha could ask, he told, "all right, I will sit and spend time with you because like I said I am gifted that I am being loved by someone. So to answer to your point, I want to set certain things right before committing to you".

Krishna's phone rang again and it was Satya. Krishna got up and went to a corner and spoke and came back and sat down, "so apparently she knows Krishna. Remember that friend I told you, stomach cancer". Radha got concerned, "oh ya, I forgot completely. How is he doing? All ok?". Krishna replied calmly, "yes, one chemo session completed, lots of nausea and vomiting. Second one is next week. I am visiting him after every session. Its really sad to see him like that. Most likely he will start loosing hair after that session". As he told that Krishna moved his fingers over his head and casually looked at his palm. There was lots of hair on his palm. His face became pale, he couldn't control his reaction. He immediately continued, "see something like this", and showed his palm to Radha and laughed. She also laughed and said, "oh Krishna, come on. Please go to the doctor and get treated". Krishna saw his palm again, rubbed it against his pant and felt very sad inside. They spent another couple of hours talking about random topics and Krishna left for Satya's place. He couldn't tell Radha anything that evening.

"Painkillers Krishna, lots of them. That's what is keeping me sane. And of course, this alcohol", told Satya as she clinked her glass against his. She was in pain and called Krishna to stay over at her place that evening. She lit a cigarette and gave one to Krishna. He denied. She was surprised, "What happened?". He said, "See, I have quit. After I came to know about my condition, I never had. I don't want this to worsen my situation. Also this is first and last drink of the day. I can sit with you all night accompanying you with juice". Satya replied, "Oh wow, Krishna that very good. I am really happy for you. Then let me also stop cigarettes". She threw hers and the packet in the dustbin. Krishna smiled and said, "don't pick it up again after I leave". She pushed Krishna away and said, "Oh Krishna, come on. I wont. I promise". She continued her drink, played some music and started dancing. He observed her and thought, "she was already feeling lonely and this dreadful disease has added so much pain. All she wanted was a simple married life", tears rolled down his eyes.

She came close to him and said, "lets dance and get rid of this pain. And also pour me another strong one". Krishna nodded his head and said, "No, enough for today". Satya replied, "I know how to make my own, so why should I depend on you. Now tell me, did you tell Radha all the details?" Krishna quietly made the drink and gave her as she continued dancing. He didn't say a word. She stopped dancing and told angrily, "so you still didn't tell her? Krishna what nonsense is this. I told you to inform her. What is wrong with you? And did you tell your parents? How are you managing at the hospital?" Krishna just sat down without looking at her. Satya started shouting at him, "Krishna, what is wrong with you? When will you tell? What are you waiting for? You already finished one session and you have another session next week. Do you even realize what you are doing? Just because you have insurance it doesn't mean the financials is taken care of right?" Krishna replied emotionlessly, "I made up a story which she is believing so far. I will tell to my sister first, she can handle all of this mess in the best possible way".

Krishna completed two sessions of chemotherapy. Vomiting and nausea stopped much earlier than the last session. He was slowly loosing his hair. It was a week past new year and Radha was back from Bengaluru. Krishna asked her to come over to a departmental store and then they decided to go to a restaurant for dinner. Krishna was looking for some new items on the shelf when Radha said, "do you know this is a new kind of packing that is coming for honey. There's no leakage". She was interrupted, "hello Krishna sir. Hope you remember me". "Oh yes, I remember. How are you sir? Oh hi Krishna, how are you?", replied Krishna. "We are fine. I met the doctor and they explained in detail. Thanks to you. We have accepted him as he is. He is very happy now. My sincere thanks to you", replied the boy Krishna's father and they left. Krishna waved at Krishna the boy, as they were leaving. Radha asked concerningly, "what happened? How do you know him? Is he that

Krishna?" Krishna replied slowly, "well… well… no, this is another Krishna. He is a homosexual and his parents didn't know about it and they consulted a doctor to understand what does it mean and thankfully they have accepted him for who he is". Radha was shocked, "oh my god, that's so sad and nice; sad because he is a homosexual but how did you know that before his parents knew? And yes, nice because his parents accepted him". Krishna replied calmly, "well, I don't think there's anything to be sad about being a homosexual. Anyway, lets leave that discussion over dinner", smiled Krishna.

As he moved to another aisle, Radha continued, "But how did you meet him?" Krishna turned to her and was lost with words and didn't know how to tell her. Just as he was about to open his mouth, he heard "hi Krishna". It took a moment for him to realize who it was. Krishna kept his hands on his face and said, "oh my god, Mumtaz, is it really you. Sorry, it took a moment for me to realize. Oh wow, what a complete makeover. You look amazing now, straightened hair and colored as well, you lost weight, and all possible saloon checklist has been ticked off. Am happy for you. Oh by the way, this is Radha, a friend of mine who is new to the city and am just taking her around". Mumtaz rushed towards him, hugged him, blushed and said, "yes, complete makeover. Thanks to you. You should come to my house now. It is completely different now from the way you saw it. I am having a great time with my husband now". She came very close to his ears and said, "I am pregnant now", and moved back and said, "he doesn't even knows about it. I am going to tell him today, we are going for dinner". She looked at Radha and said, "Radha, you have an awesome friend. He is an amazing human being. Ok I need to leave. My husband is waiting. Bye". Radha got irritated and asked, "how much more time will you take?" Krishna understood that she was angry and replied, "ok you wait in the car, I will come in ten minutes".

As Krishna was walking towards the car he saw a transgender at Radha's car asking for money. Radha was avoiding her and Krishna interrupted, "sorry, I will give". As the transgender turned, she smiled at Krishna and said, "oh Krishna, how are you?" Radha was shocked and stared at Krishna. Krishna didn't look at Radha but told the transgender, "how are you Aravind? Hope everything is alright". Aravind replied, "yes, everything is fine. Thanks to you". She looked at Radha and said, "He is a very nice person. All the best". Radha got out of the car and asked angrily, "now can you please tell me whats going on Krishna? Every time I see you are with female friends. I don't see any male friends of yours. In the last three weeks I have seen all complementing you, which is very good and even I feel good about it but you don't tell me how you know them, rather how you met them. It is not that you know these people very well. Because accidentally they meet you somewhere and thank you which means that you are possibly not in touch with them regularly. So most likely that you have met them two or three times and did something so commendable that they thank you so profusely. Am I right or wrong in my judgement so far?",

Krishna didn't look at her as she continued, "So what did you do? Now what did Mumtaz whisper to you in your ear. Why couldn't she tell it loudly". Krishna's phone rang. It was Satya. Radha saw the name on the phone. Radha's anger grew more, "Now who is this Satya. She was with you at the new year party, along with Regina and Sandhya, thats what you told me. Fine, she is a friend of yours. But why is it that she calls you continuously every time". Krishna interrupted her, "hey it is just timed incorrectly. It is happening for the second time. Otherwise she doesn't calls like this". Radha waved her hand questioningly, "ok fine, who is this transgender. How do you know her?" Krishna replied calmly, "Radha, I think you are unnecessarily getting worked up. She's just a transgender who happens to be in this area. Since my restaurant is nearby she comes around that side and happens to know my name. That's all. All transgenders bless when you give them money". Radha continued in anger, "ok agreed, so what did Mumtaz whisper to you? You have been to her house fine. You gave her tips for renovating the house, fine. You gave tips for her makeover, fine. She looks very good, fine. But why is she thanking you for all this? What did she whisper to you?" Krishna had nothing to tell, he tried avoiding that question and replied calmly, "Look Radha, we are getting late for the dinner. I will explain to you everything there. Lets go". Radha shouted, "No Krishna no. I need to know what she told you". Krishna immediately replied without giving a second thought, "She told that she was pregnant".

Radha was shocked to hear this. She kept her hands on her face and said, "what? What are you telling?" Krishna started getting irritated and replied, "so what, what is so surprising that a lady is pregnant?" Radha replied in a shocking tone, "Exactly, there is nothing so surprising that she's pregnant. But what is surprising is what she told after that, she told she didn't tell her husband and she will tell him tonight". Krishna's phone rang. It was Satya and he cut the call. He immediately got a message saying, "looks like my dream of getting married will remain unfulfilled". Radha said, "show me the message". He got more irritated and replied angrily, "what do you mean, it is personal. Why do you want to see my messages. And so what, she didn't tell her husband, it just came in a flow. It means nothing". Radha had tears and said calmly, "Krishna, you have no bloody right to get angry. You better apologize to me. Its such a big thing that she got pregnant and she's telling you first instead of her husband. Krishna, answer me straight to the point. Did you impregnate her?" "Krishna, what did Radha tell now?", asked Abhinaya.

Krishna was shocked to see Abhinaya. He put his hand on forehead and said, "sorry, I didn't come to pick you up. But what are you doing here? How did you know we were here?" Abhinaya came close to him, looked at Radha crying and held Krishna by his collar, looked angrily at him and asked, "Krishna, just answer Radha's question?" Krishna was helpless, he turned away from both of them. Radha asked, "Abhinaya, did someone named Kushboo do the interiors of his restaurant? Does he take Math tuitions part time?" Abhinaya didn't take her eyes off Krishna and replied, "I got the interiors done for the restaurant thru a friend. And this guy hates Maths". Radha cried inconsolably and said, "I knew something was wrong for the past few weeks. His over friendliness, so many female friends, which is fine, but so many compliments about him being a nice person, this message from Mumtaz, message from the boy's father". Abhinaya said, "Krishna, look at me. Its been almost a month since she proposed to you and you have still not told me about it". Radha started crying on hearing this. She kept both her hands on her forehead and started repeating as she walked in circles, "oh my god, what went wrong. Oh my god, what went wrong". Abhinaya shouted at Krishna angrily, still holding him by his collar, "Krishna, you haven't been at work regularly and I received calls from Charlie. Aunt also told me that you have stopped calling them regularly and haven't visited them in the last one month. What is happening?" Radha started shouting, "Holy shit, holy shit, now I remember, when we met for the second time I asked why was he late over a call and instead of asking me where he should come, he asked me…?"

Radha got wild and also held him by his collar. She continued, "Krishna, don't mess with me. I know exactly what you told me that night. Tell it to Abhinaya. Tell it to her damn it". Krishna didn't respond. Abhinaya removed her hands from his shirt as Radha continued to hold his collar. Abhinaya held him by his hair and turned his face towards her. That was the first time Krishna looked helplessly into Abhinaya's angry eyes. Radha asked, "Krishna, what exactly did you tell?" Krishna looked into Abhinaya's eyes and said, "which room number". Radha started crying, "Jayapradha, Kushboo, Mumtaz, Regina, Satya, Sandhya, transgender, the boy Krishna and I am the ninth". Satya called again. Both Abhinaya and Radha got a peek into his phone before he could cut the call. Radha shouted, "Show the phone, show us phone Krishna. No shit, I am not the ninth. It clearly said Satya F no. 35. What is 35 Krishna? What does it mean? You told me the other day that you save potential loyal customers number wise. Is she really your thirty-fifth friend or the thirty-fifth customer who gave you food order or is she your thirty-fifth fuck? Is it really 35 or a much higher number? Just tell one thing honestly Krishna, are you a gigolo?"

Abhinaya felt her hands greasy and as she removed her hands off his head she was shocked to see so much hair in her hands and couldn't figure out what was happening and started walking away. Radha removed her hands from his shirt, wiped her tears and walked towards her car in the other direction. Krishna ran towards Abhinaya and said with folded hands, "please wait in your car. I will come. Spend the entire evening with me and I will explain everything". And he ran towards Radha's car. She started the car and was about to move. He stood in front of the car and didn't let her move. She waited and as he came towards the driver's door, she started moving the car. He ran again towards the front of the car. She got irritated and put the air conditioner in full blast and loud music so that she could avoid hearing any sound from him. Krishna waited for a few seconds and ran towards the driver's door. But this time she didn't wait and left immediately. He realized it was no point in talking to her at that moment and ran towards Abhinaya's car. She was waiting in the passenger's seat with her usual posture, eyes closed and fingers rubbing between her eyes. He sat in the driver's seat and before he could say anything she looked into his eyes and showed her hands towards him and said in a calm tone, "Krishna, I don't want explanation just for this. I need to hear the entire story for the last six-seven months. I need to hear both sides of the story before coming to a judgement. I have the whole evening. I had a dinner meeting but I have postponed it".

Krishna kept looking at her and had tears in his eyes and said softly, "I have three things to tell you. First; do you remember you used to follow up on my stomach pain and I used to give you updates?" Abhinaya was shocked to see his tears and replied concerning, "yes, and may be the last two times I forgot about it because you told me you were fine. Now why are you crying?". Krishna continued as tears rolled down his face. He tried hard to control but couldn't. He took heavy breaths as he said, "well, there was an ultrasound….and CT scan done last month…. I …. I ….". Abhinaya couldn't understand what he was telling and had tears in her eyes as well as she had never seen him like this, and by the time she could open her mouth, he said, "I have stomach can..". By the time he could complete the last word she kept her hands on his mouth and started crying badly. She banged the dashboard of the car many times and cried loudly. Just as she stopped banging he told, "stage 3". Before he could realize she slapped him really hard that her fingers' impression could be seen on his cheeks. He didn't expect that, and it was painful. She started beating him badly, initially he resisted but later had to control her. She took a minute to calm down. Both stopped crying. Krishna continued in a slow tone, "the hair on your hands is the result of 2 chemo sessions". Abhinaya tried beating him again but he held her by her hands, she shouted at him, "Two sessions. Krishna, two fucking sessions are over and you are telling me now. And looks like you didn't tell uncle and aunt. Fucking idiot". She tried beating him continuously as she spoke and Krishna needed all his might to stop her and said, "do you want me to continue or not?" She calmed down and he left her hands.

As he kept his hands on the steering wheel he looked at Abhinaya and said, "Second, yes Radha is right, I have been a gigolo". Abhinaya slapped him hard again and this time it was even more powerful than the first one. This time Abhinaya was furious. Before Krishna could realize she took the air freshener bottle from the glove box and started beating him. He got a solid beating first before he could control her. Just as she started taking deep breaths he left her hands. She asked in an angry tone, "How many?" Krishna replied, "its been almost six or seven months." The moment he completed his sentence another unexpected slap fell on his face. Krishna became angry and held Abhinaya tightly by her shoulders and said, "Enough, its paining. Stop slapping and beating me". She shouted back at him, "Its paining for me as well fucker. For you its only physical, for me it is mental. Don't hold me tight. You bloody well know what I am asking. So answer the question to the point". Krishna left her shoulders and replied emotionlessly, "thirty nine times". Abhinaya kept her hands on her head and said, "holy shit Krishna, you slept with 39 women, fuck. Krishna what is wrong with you? Sorry, 36 women, 2 of them twice, and 1 boy. Krishna, are you a fucking pedophile?" Krishna didn't answer anything and kept looking at Abhinaya and tears rolled down his cheeks. Abhinaya shouted, "I don't know what for are you having tears". Krishna's tears continued as he said, "well Abhinaya, I always believed making others happy will make oneself happy. So I just started with that but looks like I have ended up making a big mess of myself".

Abhinaya replied to him puzzlingly, "Mess,,, it's a.big fucking mess. Do you know why drugs and prostitution is banned whereas smoking and alcohol is not. Because the former affects your mind psychologically whereas the latter are within one's control. Anyways, I really don't know what to tell. Go on, I have heard the worst possible things, I cannot expect to hear anything worse than this and you said you have a third thing to tell". Krishna replied to her, "well, you know what happened around six years ago on your birthday. Three things shattered your life and you had the ability to handle it. So obviously you can handle something like this. I am going to get married in another 55 minutes". Abhinaya was stunned to hear the last line and she kept her hands on her mouth and said, "you what in 55 minutes. Did I hear it right"? She starred at him and then at the road and then again looked at him and closed her eyes for a few seconds and then looked at him and said in a serious tone, "Radha loves you. I think you also love her. But you are marrying someone else. Are you crazy or making me crazy? Tell me every single detail possible that happened in your life for the last seven months. Every detail. If I am not convinced, I will slap you." Krishna replied, "We are going to Satya's house and I will tell you all the details as we drive. I know you don't wear gold regularly. I guess that necklace is an artificial one right, just remove it and give me. I will buy you one later". Abhinaya removed it hesitantly and asked, "what do you need this for now?" Krishna smiled and replied, "this will act as the sacred thread for the marriage".

Krishna started the car and told about everything in as much detail as possible; article he read in the paper, Karthik's meet, first customer Jayapradha and how he helped her later, Kushboo and the support he extended to her, Mumtaz and the tips he gave her, Regina and the advice he offered her, Sandhya and the vibrator he shared with her, Aravind and the other vibrator, Krishna and the enlightenment about homosexuality to his parents, three girls and the strip dance; the three incidents where he used his ingenuity in order not to get caught, and ended with Satya on how he technically lost his virginity to her without a condom. Abhinaya listened to all of this in her usual pose, fingers running between her closed eyes. She smiled many times and wiped her tears few times. She looked at him and said in an emotionless tone, "Krishna, assume I am your customer, read out the list to me". Krishna stopped the car and ensured it was on the side of the road, looked at her and said in a shocking tone, "Are you crazy? How can you? Damn it, you are my sister". She waited and kept looking at him. He engaged the gear to move the car but she applied the hand brake and held it tight. He knew that she would not budge, cleared his throat, hesitated, cleared his throat again and recited the entire roster as he would to a customer. She listened till the end, started laughing and couldn't control her laughter.

After she stopped, tears rolled down her eyes as she said, "Krishna, you were the only lovely brother that I had and you supported me wherever and whenever possible. You have the deadliest of disease and to add on to it you have been a gigolo, what have you done to yourself, Krishna?" Krishna took a deep breath, looked at her and said, "do you know how I came to know about the stomach cancer? I was sodomized by two men, so the count of 39 is actually without these two men. By the way I only kissed the boy." Krishna cried as he continued, "While checking the ultrasound for any internal injuries there was a suspicion and that's how things unraveled". Abhinaya hugged Krishna and started crying loudly. After a few seconds both stopped crying and he pushed her away.

As Krishna continued to drive he said, "Look Abhinaya, I don't know why I did all of this. I have no clue as to why and how I started. But ya, it was a surreal experience. Many women liked being licked as they never experienced it. Different women have different vaginal smells. Actually few women told me not to lick as it would smell bad". Radha interrupted him, "onset of periods". Krishna took a pause, looked at her and continued, "many like men on top because it gets very difficult the other way round for both. Many woman like being sucked on their breasts during the insertion act. Few women actually dug their nails on my back and I had to visit a skin doctor. One woman enjoyed getting her armpit licked and one woman enjoyed being licked on her butthole and one woman enjoyed giving me a fellatio. I understand that for these three women there was some physical contact. But one woman actually told me to jerk off twice and as I was completing for the second time I broke the bathroom faucet holder. Till today I am not able to understand what kind of a fetish fantasy she had seeing me jerk off. It gets really tiring always and painful occasionally as sometimes the woman gets the orgasm earlier and they are done whereas the dick is full of semen but the act is not over. If I had not been hitting the gym it would have been very difficult. I had severe back pain after certain endeavors.

The summary is this, whatever we are shown in movies is fascinating but reality is something else. And whatever we see in porn is awesome but is completely orchestrated and is bullshit, as it is done by actors and none of that is possible on a daily basis", Abhinaya laughed heartfully for the first time in the last three hours as Krishna concluded, tears ran over her cheeks as she said, "what have you done to yourself Krishna, why were you so confused in life". Krishna cried and replied, "I have made 9 people happy Abhi, that's all I did, made them genuinely happy. Unfortunately the ninth one is Radha which happened to be the other way round".

On reaching Satya's house, he picked a pair of roses from the pot outside and gave to Abhinaya, and as Satya opened the door, both Krishna and Abhinaya were shocked to see her. Satya had significant dark circles around her eyes and she looked very drowsy & tired. Krishna asked her concerningly, "hey, whats wrong with you. Everything all right. She's my sister, she knows everything and I cant hide things from her". Both the girls smiled at each other. As Satya asked them to come inside, she started crying loudly and fell on the floor. Krishna held her and both started crying. Abhinaya had tears looking at both of them. Satya cried to Krishna, "its so painful Krishna. I don't know what to do. I feel something is burning inside my body. I think my biggest wish will remain unfulfilled". Krishna held her face by his hands, looked into her eyes and replied, "marry me Satya. Lets marry now". Satya couldn't believe what she was hearing and hugged him. Both wiped their tears, Krishna started the cigarette lighter and kept it in the middle of the hall. Abhinaya handed over one rose to each of them, and both of them exchanged. Krishna took out the necklace from his pocket and put over Satya's neck. Abhinaya clapped her hands and pronounced them husband and wife. Satya had tears and just as she was about to kiss Krishna, she became conscious of Abhinaya's presence and Krishna on seeing her said, "don't bother about her. She doesn't mind all this and she keeps seeing this only when she's abroad". Abhinaya came towards both of them, pinched Krishna on his shoulder and hugged both of them. Satya started crying very badly and said, "Krishna, I need to tell you something…. It was… It was really painful for me and I couldn't bear the pain. So I took an overdose of my painkillers… I am feeling nauseated…. I … I … I will die soon..". The last words rang hard in Krishna's ears and he started crying and Abhinaya had tears too. Krishna tried consoling her to go to the hospital immediately but Satya didn't listen. Satya continued crying and said, "You fulfilled my last wish also Krishna…. Thanks… thanks a lot. I am sure you are the best for…. best for…. Radha", and breathed her last. Krishna cried inconsolably and Abhinaya hugged him.

For the next seven days Krishna was lost in thought and had teary eyes on & off. He shaved his head and went with Abhinaya to his parents' place. Upon hearing his medical condition, Krishna's father fell unconscious and his mother was heartbroken. They promised Abhinaya that they would not force anything onto Krishna and let him decide to take the right decision as and when necessary, till the treatment gets over. Later they asked Vivek to come to the restaurant. When they informed both Vivek and Charlie, both cried miserably. Later during the conversation, Krishna promised Vivek that he will support as much as he could while undergoing the treatment as his third chemotherapy session was due the next day. Immediately on hearing it, Vivek held him by the collar and said in an irritating tone, "you better get well soon. You have never taken an off ever. So better take your time off and I know how to manage with Charlie". Krishna smiled and so did Abhinaya. Charlie hugged Krishna, cried and said, "What happened Krishna, why you? I don't know how you will manage"? Krishna replied, "well Charlie, at last you will not have me around and you can work peacefully I guess" and smiled. Charlie pushed him away and smiled.

After the completion of the third chemotherapy session Krishna became very weak. He was in the hospital for more than the required number of days. Abhinaya stayed with him at the hospital and continued working from there. "This WFH is getting interesting now, considering the current COVID situation, WFH – work from hospital", said Abhinaya as both laughed. After he reached back home, Regina, Charlie and Vivek visited him on different days. The only person who was yet to know about him or see him was his 'love' Radha. Krishna tried reaching Radha many times over a call and over a message, but in vain. When Abhinaya came home he asked her again, "look, she wont talk to me, that's fine. But what stops her from talking to you". Abhinaya replied calmly, "I used my sources and found that she's moving back to Pune on March 1st, she got an internal posting and also, she wants to move before this COVID become bigger. Look Krishna, you have made a big mess of yourself with whatever you have done. Someone genuinely liked you and it would have worked well, and knowing you, you would have taken the greatest care of her and kept her happy in all possible ways". Tears rolled down Krishna's eyes, he looked away from Abhinaya and said, "that's what exactly I did. I kept all my customers happy", and closed his eyes.

Krishna kept coughing vigorously the next few days and complained of difficulty in breathing. Abhinaya got him admitted to the hospital and was shocked when the doctor told her that he has contracted COVID. He had been isolated and could only talk to people over phone. He broke down miserably when he came to know about it. As such human touch and presence matters the most during chemotherapy and this COVID worsened the situation. He had been isolated for a week and his parents nor Abhinaya could even see him. Abdul also came back after an assignment and tried to use his influence to meet Krishna but nothing worked. Krishna's situation worsened and was put on a ventilator as his oxygen levels dropped. The reports mentioned that his lungs were filled with the virus. The doctors tried hard but Krishna breathed his last on the Sunday morning, the day Radha left for Pune. As she left the city and his life forever, Krishna left everyone.

Chapter 8
FINALE

"She was standing with both the legs and hands crossed and trying to look thru the corner of the eye. Both their hearts were pulsating fast, both were unable to look at each other straight and both were hesitantly coming close to each other. He removed his clothes, put on his condom and came very close to her and smooched her. That was first time she looked straight into his eyes. There was shock and a flash of fear on her face. He got concerned and asked, "are you alright?" Her lips were trembling and she started sweating. He got scared and held her tight over her shoulders and with a louder tone asked, "are you ok? shall I leave?". She said, "lets lie down"", Radha read the text in a confident tone to a small audience in a book shop. "Lets keep the next set of lines for your private study", said Radha to the audience and smiled, and all laughed. Her dream of writing a book was successfully achieved. After Krishna's demise, when Abhinaya broke the news to Radha, she cried inconsolably. They had a long call where Abhinaya gave all the details of Krishna. Radha had a mix of emotions throughout the call. After the book reading session, a few took autographs from Radha and a few posed with her for a selfie. One of the persons from the audience came and introduced herself as Regina and cried. For a moment Radha couldn't understand and suddenly it struck her that it was the old lady who helped Krishna with his injury. Radha's eyes filled with tears but she controlled herself. She took out a piece of paper from her bag and showed it to Regina, it read, "Abhinaya, please give all my notes and details to the love of my life, Radha. Hope this will help her fulfill her dream of writing a book". Radha smiled and said, "Little did I realize that during his last days he was telling me about himself and not about his friend. exactly two years ago he left us on this same day and I wanted to release the book on the same day". Regina said, "I actually finished the online version in one sitting. I came to know about it thru Abhinaya. Is she around?" Radha replied, "Actually she couldn't make it as she's not in town. Well, sorry, I thought I actually changed the names in order to protect the individual's privacy. My bad, I missed yours".

Regina smiled and replied, "well, I was actually amused when I read about myself. You have captured my entire conversation with Krishna really well. A lot of thought has gone into the book. And for the privacy part, don't bother. I am not staying here anymore. I have actually moved to Coimbatore. I have found an interesting partner. I came over to Chennai for a couple of days to accompany him for his personal work. Coincidentally your book reading event happened. Anyway, I need to leave. Take care". Radha was surprised to hear that and replied, "oh nice. I am happy for you. Looks like you followed Krishna's advice. I contacted most of them, every individual who followed Krishna's advice are happier than before. Hope people with similar issues can think about it when they read this book. Take care".